To
Mac + Sue
Hope you enjoy
Love Colin x

Colin Mitchell

Colin was born in Wednesbury in the West Midlands in 1948. The seventh child, and the youngest of his family, born to his mother and father, Frances and Stephen Richards Nicholls. He attended Joseph Edward Cox Primary School on the Friar Park Estate Wednesbury and then Charlemont Secondary Modern. It was not until this new millennium that Colin had the opportunity to attend University, thanks to the kindness and belief shown in him by the Head of English, Prof. David Roberts, at the University of Central England Birmingham. Here he successfully gained a 2:1 Honours degree in English Language/Literature and there has since been no holding him back.

Colin is now retired but his last four working years were spent at Hall Green Primary School where he thoroughly enjoyed the work that he did there with the children. He appreciated the value that both staff and children seemed to place upon him. Colin always held the love of and the aspirations/achievement of the child paramount.

Since losing his mother at the start of this new millennium he has created new opportunities in life. His only regret is that his parents were unable to live to see this progress.

By the same author

In My Mind's Eye (United Press) 2006
ISBN 13 978 1 84436 157 1

The Turn Of The Worm (Vanguard Press) 2007
ISBN 978 1 84386 355 7

Star Gazey Boy (Vanguard Press) 2008
ISBN 978 1 84386 427 1

Scrooby 'The Pilgrim Fathers' (Vanguard Press) 2008
ISBN 978 1 84386 470 7

Time and a Third (Vanguard Press) 2009
ISBN 978 1 84386 8

Bostin Fittle (Vanguard Press) 2009
ISBN 978 1 84386 871 2

The Decline of Josh White

Colin J Nicholls

The Decline of Josh White

Vanguard Press

VANGUARD PAPERBACK

A CIP catalogue record for this title is available from the British Library.

ISBN 978 1 84386 806 4

Vanguard Press is an imprint of Pegasus Elliot Mackenzie Publishers Ltd.
www.pegasuspublishers.com

First Published in 2013

Vanguard Press
Sheraton House Castle Park
Cambridge England

Printed & Bound in Great Britain

I would like to dedicate this third novel to my sister Brenda and her husband Gordon Wilkins, for being there for me. For as long as I can, or wish to, remember, Brenda was there as my big sister; she was the youngest of three sisters and the one I remember mostly growing up alongside. She shared a bedroom with two brothers and me when we were children and she was always there when I was in any sort of need and I still feel that she is today. If I was ever in any doubt about anything, I could guarantee that both Brenda and Gordon were there to encourage me and they were usually the first ones to sample my work. I don't believe that I could guarantee a genuine opinion off either of them though, because I do believe that they saw no fault in me, and I genuinely value everything they did for me, so a huge thank you.

For Brenda

Brenda sadly passed away on the 7th of August 2008. She bravely fought and suffered for many years with cancer. The grief of losing her is unbearable. I am not usually stuck for words but I cannot find the words sufficient enough to express satisfactorily my love for her in order to give it justice.

Taken from *Forever To Be Mine* (Time and a Third)
'Will youth be ours forever more
And pleasant warm sunshine?
To have and hold whom I adore
Forever to be mine.'
Love you forever

Colin xx

Acknowledgements

I would again like to say a big THANK YOU to:
Natalie and Paul Newman,
(My niece and her husband)

For all of the hard work that they have dedicated in the proofreading of this, my latest novel. Recent times have not been the best of our lives and therefore I truly appreciate everything that they have done for me.

God bless you both.

Foreword

'The Decline of Josh White' is my third novel and my seventh published work. It is a wide departure from my previous novel, 'Scrooby – The Pilgrim Fathers'. It has a serious subject matter of death, drugs and abuse – to say any more than this would be giving too much of the plot away. I enjoyed the freedom I experienced in the writing of the purely fictional 'Turn of The Worm', and became only too aware of the restrictions that a non-fictional storyline can place upon the freedom of imagination when I was writing 'Scrooby – The Pilgrim Fathers'. This latest offering has given me back my freedom and allowed me to once more open up my mind.

In the white heat of love and the close coupling of passion it can be extremely easy to become oblivious to the existing world and the consequences of your actions. 'Josh White' is an average child of his day, caught up in the desires of the individual and subsequently the eventual collapse of the family. In the society that he lives in, it appears to have become too easy to underestimate the determination of one's own isolated actions at the expense of the extended unit. The domino effect can lead to a landslide and thus the downfall of all reliant and subservient attachments, leading to total destruction.

Contents

CHAPTER ONE

Dereliction

His body wrenched violently in uncontrollable spasms. A body that was twisted and in decay. Saliva dribbled from the corner of his gaping mouth, saturating the rags beneath his head and causing his long, matted hair to stick in strands across his face. The occasional indecipherable murmuring gurgled from his throat as he lay there, in that inhuman state, befitting only the rats that inhabit the stinking sewers.

The house was a back-to-back terrace situated in the suburbs of Birmingham. All of the windows were boarded over with plywood sheets; all screwed and secured tightly, too late to have saved the shattered glass of the windows. This was still spread across the floor within. There was also a ply panel that once firmly secured the entrance door that had now been left insecure against the locking jamb. Through this closing side a hole had been crudely pierced and a length of string passed through; this string was bound within around and around a bent six-inch nail that had been hammered firmly into the jamb. Directly inside, besides the shards of glass upon the floor, lay piles of unopened mail, circulars, and sheets of old newspapers, dirty rags, broken wood and strips of wallpaper long since ripped from the walls. The blackened lead grate, the original focus of this tiny hovel, stood cold with ash spilling outwards across the hearth; once the focus for gathered friends, it now presented itself as a symbol of gloom. The kitchen door was no longer there and the built-in tongue and groove cupboard over in the one corner was minus its drawers and doors probably long since burnt upon the fire. In the other corner the stairway door lay ajar as if to beckon you upwards.

The narrow staircase still had remnants of the red and white chequered lino that once brightened its treads. It was very dark and gloomy and the smell from within unpleasantly flared and irritated the nostrils. On the landing there was just one entrance, again missing a door. This led directly into a pokey little bedroom that was pierced by lances of light which penetrated the intermittent gaps around the ply sheet across the window; enough to illuminate old papers and a pile of bottles thrown into one of the corners. It also lit the way through to another door surprisingly still intact and almost closed. Behind this door a ladder-back chair had been strategically placed, propped against the doorknob to keep the door in this position. Once passed this obstruction, the spangled sunrays gave light to a double mattress that lay upon the bare wooden boards, pushed against the rear wall. The stench here was the source of that which filled the stagnant, cold moist air that hung heavily within the stairwell. Stuffing sprang sporadically from the holes torn within this mattress and a bundle of old rags and coats covered some of its upper surface. Again the floor held more torn papers, discarded bottles, sweet wrappers and mouse droppings. There was an old lead grate across the one corner of the room within touching distance of the bed. It like the living room fire, bore the remains of previous life but now lay dead and ash strewn. Next to the mattress there were a few cast-off hypodermic needles. The walls, previously and no doubts lovingly whitewashed many times over, were now smeared with blood, excrement, graffiti and other violations. In places, the plaster had fallen and the exposed laths were showing, bearing an uncanny resemblance to the ribs of the malnourished. The ceiling that was once a nice tone of cream eggshell was now a dowdy grey only occasionally brightened by the black and green moulds that grew enthusiastically upon the surface, dampened from the leaking slates above. In the centre a twin marooned flex dropped from its porcelain rose minus its lamp holder, around which the flies did turns before settling upon it. Dust lay upon dust and cobwebs linked ceiling to wall. A strong smell of urine permeated the other unpleasant odours.

The pile upon the mattress rolled from side to side violently and low murmurings stirred. Suddenly the top layer was cast aside; an emerging head shot forward and vomit was strenuously propelled across the floor. Like a tortoises head on the recoil this head retreated back from whence it came. The flies around the light pendant descended rapidly like the red arrows in neat formation, and settled upon easy pickings. The body beneath the pile had lain there for who knows how long? For it certainly did not, or should I say, what was left of it did not know. A life lived within a semi-to-fully unconscious stupor. Days, weeks, months, who really cared? Life passed on by and survived surprisingly well without the contribution of the derelict heap. In fact it had done now, for the last two years or more, although the body beneath knew nothing of this. This house was just the present residence of many of its kind that had passed before it; one dilapidated property after another, one filthy slum looking much like the last and long overdue its demolition.

For several days now the mattress had been this body's solace; a body too weak to lift itself much above its horizontal level. This particular bout of unconsciousness was the result of a fortunate find amongst the skips dotted along the terraces; that led to a lucky sale in the park and therefore meant sufficient funding for the latest fix. As for food well that had not passed these lips for a few days before this last spell of drugged indulgence took its toll. Before this the lunch box had mainly been cylindrical, black and plastic with the only other exception being green, oblong and alloy, this stood behind the China Plate café. Now we were far beyond malnutrition. A shadow of his former self this was, 'Josh White'. Totally unrecognisable as the once happy-go-lucky, talented athletic schoolboy, who had once taken, on his last school sports day, the 100 metres, the long jump and the 400 metres relay medals. If his relay partners could see this wasted body now; well they would probably go into severe denial of ever having known him. He was, at that time, a little less than ten stone of upright, taught and toned muscle. Now he would probably struggle to register six stone wringing wet.

Josh's life lay precariously upon a balance; slowly tipping in the wrong direction. No one he had previously known knew where he was now, and he presumed that not one of them cared either. As far as he was aware not one person besides the Old Bill had ever set out in search of him. He preferred the state of unconsciousness to the reality of living because whilst he was in this state he was oblivious to all. When semi-conscious he still had the nightmares of his unpleasant past; nightmares that caused him to roll and sweat and toss and turn, screeching out violently into the never-ending silent nights. He was aware that those screeches could lead to his detection and this caused him the greatest concern that he may one day be found and taken back to face reality. Josh lived an ugly, isolated, lonely existence. His last normal conversation with a servant of society had been about a week earlier when, having been discovered by a friendly environmental inspector, who had entered the building to confirm security and vacancy, it had been suggested that he must leave with some urgency. This inspector had tried to coax Josh back into existence within the outer world. He had immediately recognised the lad's vulnerability and had nothing but good intentions. He tried to plead with Josh, explaining to him the dangers that he faced. The terraces faced imminent demolition. A great leaded ball would be used to erase them from the sight of humanity forever and it was his responsibility to ensure the health and safety of the public. Unfortunately for this well-intentioned man, Josh saw a great leaded ball as a reasonable option amongst his present choices in life, and those were but a few.

Josh drifted in and out of consciousness; occasionally he tasted the unpleasantness within his mouth; tastes that were similar to that of the burnt scrapings of an overheated saucepan. Sometimes he became aware that he was lying in damp although he recognised little of the awful smells that choked the air about him. The discomfort from his twisted back and the uncleanliness of his body were only upon the rare occasion evident to him. It was only when he decided to adjust his position that he had felt discomfort. This was sufficient to make him wince loudly. Changing his position was seldom anything that he would be aware of because he retained very little knowledge of the comforts of life. His body would occasionally enter upon a convulsion; a chain reaction to the abdominal pains caused from the pangs of hunger and probably the state of his rotting gut. Ulcers lined the interior of his mouth and his teeth and tongue were, by now, sufficiently coated with sufficient plaque and mushy fungal growth to disguise any recognition of tooth decay. He gulped occasionally in order to collect any remaining spittle that might quench his desperate thirst.

Should he ever be conscious enough to recollect anything of his previous life, retained within the shell that was once his brain, then, this would only act to drive him into a frantic search for the black hole from whence he had emerged. An occasional blip of pleasant memory might fleet across his internal eye; this occurring about as often as the presence of a street light in the Gobi Desert. The latter memories lasted no longer than a millisecond and bore no real resemblance to him of his own experience of life. Josh was on a quest that led only to ultimate damnation. He no longer had a purpose. He saw no light at the end of this never-ending tunnel. In fact he saw only the tunnel gradually closing in upon him, collapsing about his head and burying him alive. His quest seemed only now to suffocate upon the stench of a decaying body. If there was a God why did he continue to make submission such a difficult process?

Josh's 21st birthday had recently come and gone. He had been totally oblivious to it. There was no cake, no presents, no visiting friends or relatives, no key-cards, no long lingering kisses, no cheques and no cars. Just as his 19th and 20th birthdays had been, total nonentities. In fact, should he have either interest or faculty, Josh would have extreme difficulties in recollecting when, or upon which previous birthday, he had last received a gift or fond wishes. Christmasses? Well what about them? What interest of Christmas is shown by the living dead? If Josh still had any grasp upon the ways of humanity, which he did not, then what good would the occasional gesture of goodwill have meant to him? Christmas, birthdays, bullshit!

Cold shivers ran up and down his body, and pains pierced his skull. Cramps ran through his legs. Unwittingly he urinated, and felt no discomfort; just the warmth between his thighs, a somewhat pleasant feeling for the short few moments that it lasted. Something choked his throat, causing him to gasp and rasp, as it gathered together in one restrictive lump. He collected this together and pushed it slowly out onto his lips until it slowly crept unapprehended across the stubble of his chin. A violent pain stabbed him mightily within his chest, his arms ached naggingly and again his throat restricted. His legs drew up sharply and involuntarily towards the pit of his stomach. His eyes rolled and he cried out, but there was no one there in the darkness, he had no one to comfort him.

CHAPTER TWO

15 Years Earlier

Josh sat behind a huge Coca-Cola; he had six candle flames dancing merrily before him. They twisted and turned slightly, caused by the light breeze that was entering in through the wide opened patio doors. There were screams of joy, enthusiasm and encouraging words around him.

"Come on Josh, blow them all out!"

"Make a wish!"

"Hurry it up Josh, I'm starving!"

"Come on Josh, 1-2-3!"

Josh inhaled sharply and exhaled with the same sharpness, pppphhhhhh!

The candles extinguished and everyone cheered. Josh's Dad patted him lovingly upon the head and his Mom planted a big wet kiss upon his cheek, which he quickly brushed aside with the sleeve of his shirt. Josh's best friend, Liam, sat at his side and he squealed with delight.

Josh decided immediately that this was the best birthday that he had ever had. He still had presents to open; he had already opened the ones he had received from his Mom and Dad, they had been all that he had wished for. He had a magic set, an operation game, three books and his favourite toy of all time, 'Robbo the walking Robot'. He had filled himself with cakes, jelly and ice cream, and now he was being handed the first cut and the largest slice of his blue and white foot-ball cake. Liam received the second slice and he thanked Mrs White for it before rapidly sinking his teeth sharply within its centre. Liam and Josh had met at nursery school when they were both four; they had started on the same day and immediately bonded. Two whole years had passed by. Now at six years of age they were virtually inseparable; excepting that they actually lived two miles apart, so this meant that outside of school, Josh or Liam's Mom had to make special visits to bring the two together during holidays or at weekends.

Mrs White offered the next slice of birthday cake across the table towards Pearl, Josh's sister, but as she reached out for it Trevor, the elder brother, snatched it from his mother's hands and laughed aloud, taunting his younger sister. His Mother scolded him,

"Trevor! You naughty, naughty lad! You know that that was meant for your sister, now apologise."

Trevor sat there unmoved by his Mother's words or his sister's tears. He quickly and deliberately nibbled all around the outer edge of the cake and grinned causing Frank White to clip him sharply at the back of his left ear. Trevor did not even flinch; he merely continued to consume the cake. Mrs White quickly cut another slice and offered it into Pearl's hands. Her tears ceased and she too began to eat.

Pearl was blonde haired and blue eyed with delicate skin. She was small boned and had a greater resemblance to her Mother than either of the lads. She was four years older than Josh and two years younger than her selfish brother Trevor. This being Josh's sixth birthday, Pearl was now ten years of age and Trevor twelve. Josh, in contrast to Pearl, was mousey haired and had a darker skin complexion, as did Trevor but he had jet-black wavy hair. It was not just their appearances that helped to individualise this trio as Trevor's attitude and behaviour set him apart from the other two. Trevor could at times be hard, mean and nasty. Out of sight or hearing of either parent he took great enjoyment from taunting or bullying his brother and sister. For Pearl, being the closest to Trevor's age, meant that she was mostly the one to suffer at his hands. If any of Pearl's most prized or loved possessions went missing, or were broken, then usually Trevor was involved in one way or another. Mrs White regularly found herself scolding Trevor and warning him of his fate upon his father's return home. It had become almost routine; following a kiss and a greeting, for her to be informing Mr White of Trevor's latest grim escapades. His Dad must have grown weary of the amount of times he had needed to read Trevor the riot act. Mostly, these warnings appeared to fall upon deaf ears, and Trevor had become more cunning and adept as the years had progressed. He was also aware of his dad's lack of willingness to enforce any real punishment upon any of them.

Josh was young and a little oblivious to a lot of the aforementioned occurrences, but he too had his set-toos with his brother. Trevor's attitude had the result in distancing him more and more from his parents. It is fair to say that if parents can have favourites, then Pearl was Mrs Whites and Josh was Mr White's. In reality, and for most of the time, they loved each of their children in equal measure but at the worst of times to varying degrees. This now could possibly have been one of those times, because Trevor suddenly lunged across the table and took a firm grip upon Robbo the Robot. Mr White, with the deftest of touches, moved in unison taking a firm grip upon Trevor's wrist with a strong right hand, causing Trevor to wince and loosen his hold. Swiftly with his left hand, he took back Robbo and returned it to its rightful owner.

"Come on, let's pass the parcel!" Mrs White suggested.

"Yes!" cried out Pearl as she grabbed Josh's hand helping him from the table and Liam quickly followed on behind them.

"I won't play, it's for kids," sneered Trevor.

"Then don't play," said Mrs White, frustrated by Trevor's attitude. "It's only you who'll miss out on the fun."

Trevor remained in his seat, sour faced and unperturbed. All the others sat in a ring around the floor whilst Mrs White set up the music.

Have you ever noticed how the music during pass the parcel always seems to stop at the most worthy of recipients; you know the youngest or the celebrated? Intriguing isn't it? Well, in this instance the music first stopped for Pearl to receive the parcel. She hastily unwrapped one layer and when the music recommenced, she passed it on. It then reached Josh before stalling, and he began to tear at the paper but still having not located the prize, he again passed it onwards with the recommencement of the music. Two more full circles were achieved and the parcel rested with Liam as the music ceased. He frantically unwrapped it to discover a comic and some sweets. Several parcels later, both Pearl and Josh had received gifts too. In fact Josh, the birthday boy, had received two lots. Maybe the second was intended for Trevor, who throughout the proceedings had continued to ignore everyone, sitting contentedly at the table eating sausages off sticks.

Mr White then decided that they should all go out into the garden for a while, it being such a nice day, and he grabbed a small football from the linen basket on his way out. The garden was made up of a fair-sized lawn surrounded by borders all lying just beyond the paved patio. At the top end of the garden there was an old wooden shed. This was full of the usual junk, plus household maintenance and garden tools. Beyond this shed there was an old brick built garage with an asbestos sheet roof, although Frank White had never owned or learnt how to drive a car. The garage made good storage for his and the children's bicycles. There were also a few items of discarded furniture, cardboard boxes, bags of garden waste (ready for the tip), hula-hoops and assorted less popular toys.

On the lawn there was a small tubular framed goal. Liam immediately ran between the posts, considering himself to be a bit of a goalkeeper. Trevor had wandered out half-heartedly behind them, he carried with him his basketball, this he began to bounce and shoot hoops in the ring that had been fixed by his father, upon the rear wall of the house. The Sun was extremely bright; it was a very hot day. Shortly afterwards they were joined outside by Mrs White and Liam's Mother. They sat down on the bench beneath the sunshade both sipping something from long slender glasses. Occasionally the ball came their way and they either threw it, or kicked it, back in the general direction of the group. Eventually the sun and the fast pace grew too much for Pearl, and she joined the ladies upon their bench. Her fair skin was red and her Mother quickly went inside to fetch some sun cream.

Trevor was a tall well built lad, not heavy or overweight but muscular. He was skilful with the basketball and continually dropped the ball through the hoop. Mrs Hullstone sat watching him for a while waiting for Florence to return, and she shouted across to Trevor to congratulate him upon his prowess but he simply ignored her. Florence had just returned through the rear doors and had just caught Mrs Hullstone's words. She immediately rebuked Trevor for being so ignorant, telling him that he had been spoken to politely and that he ought not to ignore Mrs Hullstone in the way that he just had. Trevor never even turned his head but continued to do exactly what he wanted to do. Just then, Frank came across to Florence and kissed her softly upon the cheek. Then he stole her glass swiftly from her hands and took a big drink. Mrs Hullstone just giggled but Florence snatched it back out of his grasp and told him to go get his own. She then said that he should not be ignoring Trevor's bad behaviour in the way that he had. Mr White was unaware of what had happened but he went across to Trevor to speak with him. Frank, being the type of person that he was, and catching Trevor totally oblivious to his presence, nipped in to a rebounding ball, bounced it around the surprised Trevor and then netted it in one. Trevor pushed his Dad harmlessly upon the shoulder and Frank pushed him back. Then they tussled for a few moments and finished up rolling about in the grass. Both were laughing their heads off. Florence shouted, "I didn't mean that you should behave in the same way that he does."

She intended no malice and it was nice to see, for just a few moments, that Trevor was still his Dad's lad. The youngsters, having heard what was happening, and seeing the couple upon the grass, immediately ran over and jumped on top of them.

"Somebody's going to get hurt! Now pack it in Frank!" shouted Florence.

At least Trevor's face had cracked, as he sat there showing a big grin upon it, ruffling his brother's hair whilst holding him about the shoulders. Frank got up and walked back over to the ladies but the lads continued with their tussle.

Florence loved Frank indescribably. She also loved her children, house and lifestyle. Frank picked up Pearl from the bench, lifted her up high then sat in her place upon the bench placing her upon his lap. Florence began to rub in the sun cream.

"I don't know who the biggest kid is; you or them!"

"She should have had that done before she came out here," said Frank.

"I know but you're always too quick off the mark."

Pearl took her Dad's glasses from his face and put them

on herself. Mrs Hullstone laughed loudly.

"You're too much like your Mom for even your Dad's glasses to make you look like him," she said.

Frank took his glasses back and then pretended to steal Pearl's nose from her face, holding his thumb between his forefingers and then planting it back. He stood up and went back into the kitchen, returning shortly afterwards with a beer. He sat down next to Pearl and she swiftly stole his glass and took a mouthful.

"You owe me that one," she said.

Trevor untangled himself from the grasp of the other lads and went across to the kitchen; he returned holding a large chunk of pork pie and three sausages. He came over to the bench and sat on the grass alongside his Mother. He reached out to offer her a sausage but she declined. Then, seemingly in an effort to repair his bad behaviour and redeem himself, he offered Mrs Hullstone the same sausage, a sort of a peace offering. She accepted and so all was well. Trevor's age and puberty seemed recently to be affecting his behaviour, sometimes he could appear to be hard and uncaring, but he was still not a bad lad at heart.

Josh and Liam had gone back to their football. Liam was again in goal and Josh was taking pot shots at him. The two of them were great friends and had been since the day that they had first met. Never once had there been an argument or ill feeling expressed between them. Liam had once stopped at the White's for a whole week, whilst Mrs Hullstone had been in hospital, so he always felt at home. Neither of them had other friends; they seemed content with each other's company. There wasn't anything that they did not share; oh, accept fishing. Liam occasionally went fishing with his Dad although Josh was always invited but it had never appealed to him. The age gap between Josh and Trevor set them apart most times so Liam was a surrogate brother. Josh was also close to his sister Pearl, closer than to Trevor that is. Trevor distanced himself a little from the pair of them. At this time Josh and Pearl still shared a bedroom; as they had done since Josh had left his parent's bedside. So Trevor had his own domain, a bedroom with pop-stars and footballers adorning the walls. There had recently been family disputes every time it had been simply suggested that at some point or other, Trevor and Josh would have to share. Trevor had become independently established and he did not take the suggestion kindly. The only other alternative was that the small junk-room (cupboard) should be cleared and may just about take a single bed. This might have to be a compromise that Josh would have to make, but he was all for it!

The boys returned to their Mother's sides, sweat pouring from their brows and started sipping hastily upon their cokes. Mrs Hullstone suggested that it was time for her and Liam to leave. Josh did not want Liam to go but his Mother reassured him that they would be seeing a lot more of each other throughout the summer holiday. Mrs Hullstone had offered an open invitation for them to go over at any time during the week. In fact, on the following Friday they were all going to the zoo together. Mrs White and Josh accompanied the Hullstones to the front door. Josh and Liam hugged, as did the Mothers and they said their farewells.

When they returned into the rear garden they found Mr White discussing the possibility of a holiday in the following year. Frank had always wanted to go to Cornwall.

"But how would we get there?" Trevor asked.

"By train. Just because we don't have a car doesn't mean we can't go places, you know."

"I know, but we never do, do we?"

Florence, realising what the conversation was about,

butted in.

"Trevor, that's unfair. We don't go on big holidays but we do get about don't we?"

Trevor returned to the idea of travelling by train.

"How long would it take by train Dad?"

"Oh, I don't know, Trevor, but I'll find that out, however long it takes we'll get there."

"Where's Cornwall Dad?" asked Josh.

His Mom replied, "Oh it's a good way Josh. Are you sure about this Frank?"

"We'll have to find out, but you know how many times I've mentioned this before and now I really would like to take the kids before they get too old, especially Trevor."

"But where would we stay?" she asked.

"I'll find out some details, but remember, I said next year not this, so don't all keep moaning on at me will you?"

That night they all went to bed with thoughts of their best ever family holiday in their minds. 'What would Cornwall be like?' Trevor kept thinking. Would his Dad keep his word? Could they really afford it? The kids all realised that Dad would be out early to work in the morning, so there would be no opportunity to continue their discussion. Would he have said anything else to Mom? Or would she just tell them to be patient? Josh dreamt of his birthday; his cake, his presents and his friend. He slept contented and so did Pearl, who, since she had slipped under the bed covers he had not heard one peep from. In all the time he had shared Pearl's room, Josh had come to accept that Pearl slept like a log.

CHAPTER THREE

Cornwall

It was five minutes before the train was due to leave; they had the compartment to themselves. They occupied six seats; Mr & Mrs White, Trevor, Josh, Pearl and Liam. Liam's Mom had agreed for him to go on holiday with the Whites and was anxiously standing upon the platform with Mr Hullstone waiting for the train's departure. Liam and Josh pressed their faces closely against the window, flattening their noses and steaming the glass. Trevor sat next to his Dad discussing the adventure and what they might get up to. Mrs White was still fussing over Pearl; straightening her coat and tidying her hair. Suddenly the whistle blew and the train shunted forward, gasping as it went; steel screeching upon steel. Mr & Mrs Hullstone smiled and waved through the window and everyone inside returned these gestures.

Mr White believed that the journey might take seven or eight hours and knew that they had to change once at Plymouth. He kept reminding Floss. "Just in case he dozed off," he said. For now, he and Trevor were chatting about the new football season that started in just four weeks' time. The Albion had been reorganising during closed season and had, so far, bought four new players. Liam and Josh continued to stare out from the train, watching passing scenery, searching constantly for cows, sheep, horses or pigs. Mrs White and Pearl both read their girlie magazines to pass the time away.

"How will we know when we're in Plymouth, Dad?"

asked Josh.

"We'll know Josh, don't worry."

"Every time we stop they shout out the name of the station, cloth ears!" Trevor said sarcastically.

"Where are we now then Big Ears?" replied Josh.

"Exeter, and watch it, unless you want a smacking!" snapped Trevor.

"Don't you start, you two," said Mrs White, peering out above her *Woman's Own*.

"Is it much further Mom?" enquired Pearl.

"I don't know. Is it much further Frank?"

"Don't you start, you're as bad as the kids!"

"I ain't asked before, have I? Are we more than halfway?"

"Yes, we're more than half-way, be patient."

"You got anything else to eat Mom?" asked Josh.

"Yes, pork pie, sandwich or chocolate."

"Pork pie please."

"How about you, Liam?"

"I'll have the same please, Mrs White."

"What chocolate have you got, Mom?" enquired Trevor.

"Let's see, *Kit Kat* or *Fry's* boys."

"I'll have both."

"You'll have one or the other and be satisfied," said Mr White.

Mrs White was just handing out the food when the trolley came rattling down the corridor, offering teas and cold drinks. Frank without need of prompting jumped up and ordered something for each one of them.

They changed at Plymouth, losing only twenty minutes, and it wasn't long before they were crossing a huge steel bridge that looked out across the estuary on one side and the sea on the other. They'd never seen anything like this before; so dramatic, such a large scale, banks sweeping down to the choppy waters. Liam shouted out when he saw a sign that read, 'You are now leaving Devon and entering Cornwall.' Frank stood up and pointed outwards,

"Look, can you see that?"

Everyone clamoured around the window.

"What is it, Dad?" asked Josh.

"It's an aircraft carrier, ain't it Dad?" suggested Trevor

"It is and look, there's a Destroyer and see that there, look." He pointed towards the banks. "Just there, that's a submarine."

"There's two of them Frank, look there," added Floss.

"Wow!" Both of the young lads sighed together.

There were also countless yachts, sailing to and fro, but every one of them overlooked these because never before had any seen such warships so close at hand. The train crossed very slowly before speeding up as it cut through between two hills on the other side. The last thing that they could see, as they strained their necks to look back, was a small beach on the edge of the estuary on the Cornish side. There was just a lone man and his dog walking there.

It was 6.30pm when the train eased into Goonhaven station. It was a tiny little place compared with many of the others that they had seen on the journey. By now the train had emptied of many of its passengers and was lingering longer at every stop.

"This it Dad, Chapel Porth?"

"Yes, this is the station we want, son." replied Frank.

They pulled their luggage from above their heads and below the seats and left the compartment. The doors stood open waiting for them. Outside, there stood just one man upon the platform; he was dressed in an olive green uniform and had a flat peaked cap pressed down firmly upon his head. He had the letters, S.W.R. upon his breast pocket; he was a large round, red-faced man and very jolly looking.

"Evenin' me handsomes," were the first words that he uttered!

"Goonhaven!" followed.

No one, except Frank, knew where they were actually stopping for the week. For some unknown reason he had kept it from them all.

They knew that Goonhaven was their destination and that their Dad had spoke of Chapel Porth but that was about it. Frank put down his cases and rummaged deep into his top pocket. He pulled out some papers and unfurled them in front of the jolly, red-faced man.

"Oh, I see sir, yes sir, 'tis nice to meet you," said the man.

"Where do we go from here?" enquired Florence, tired and slightly irritable.

"Just a minute Ma," Frank replied.

"William!" shouted the station man.

"William!"

A tall thin man with a handlebar moustache dressed exactly the same as Mr Jolly, peered through the station door. The train spluttered and pulled away, rasping behind them. This left just the small group standing there alone, quietly, in what appeared to be the middle of nowhere. Mr Jolly showed the moustached man the papers that he had taken from Mr White's hands.

"Oh yes me handsomes, come with me, if you please."

They all wrestled with the baggage and followed on behind this wiry-legged individual as he swiftly, without further ado, about-turned and marched them off through the station doors. They went in, and out of the other side entrance, down a short flight of steps and out onto the track. This had flat platforms of wood placed between the two open rails making it an even surface to walk upon.

"Where we going?" Liam asked Josh.

"I don't know," replied Josh.

On the opposite side to the station position, out of their original sight, there stood four rail carriages. 'Mr Moustache', formally known as William, took them to the rear of the line of carriages and stood in front of the end carriage doorway. He pulled at a steel link chain that was hanging slightly lower than a fine, silver looking chain, which was clipped to a button and was supporting a smart pocket watch, and slid from his waistcoat pocket a long thin key upon a brass tally.

"This is it me handsomes, 'The Cornish Maiden'," he proudly announced.

He inserted the steel key into the door lock, twisted it sharply and pushed heavily upon the door.

"It sticks a bit sometimes," he turned and said to Frank, pushing the key into the palm of his hands.

It smelt of Dettol inside. The man entered and turned to beckon everyone forwards. It was nice inside; it wasn't set out, as a train carriage normally would be. To their surprise it had sofas and winged chairs, a table and benches and carpets. The man led them through; there was a kitchen, a toilet and three bedrooms.

"Is that okay then sir? Now if there's any assistance you need, any at all, then we're just across the platform, twenty-four hours of the day, sir."

He ripped from the paper that Frank had passed to him earlier, a narrow strip of paper, and handed the remaining paperwork back to him.

"How do we get off the station?" asked Frank.

"Oh 'tis me oversight, begging yer pardon, sir."

He stepped outside the carriage with Frank in pursuit and pointed to a gated opening through the adjacent hedge way.

"Through the gate sir, there's the roadway and a bus stop. Chapel Porth is no more than ten minutes' walk to the right, across the stile and fields that lie opposite, and St Agnes, perhaps twenty minutes by bus."

Mr White thanked him and William departed.

Back inside the carriages, Floss was already organising things. Pearl was filling the kettle from the sink-tap and the lads had claimed for themselves the far end carriage, this had one single bed and bunk beds. They were unpacking their clothes and arguing about drawers and cupboards. There was no argument about the beds; with these they were content. Josh had always wanted to sleep in a top bunk bed, Liam was happy below him and Trevor had his own single as he did at home.

Mrs White, seeing Frank's return, asked, "Is there a shop, Frank?"

"Oh! He didn't say and I never asked, do we need stuff then?"

"No, not yet but we will do."

"That's alright then, we'll sort that out later."

"This is real nice Frank, where did yer find out about this then?"

"Harry Middleton at work Ma. He said he knew of someone who'd been here, and he said how good it was. It is nice isn't it, a bit quiet but well equipped."

"Can't turn the stove on Mom!" shouted Pearl.

Frank went to her assistance and immediately realised that it was gas and there was no gas coming through.

"Turn it back off, Pearl, and wait till I say so, okay?"

He went outside and reappeared alongside the kitchen carriageway window. Floss stood and watched, she heard clanking and saw Frank give the thumbs up, and then he returned. As he entered he said, "Try that Pearl."

He stood and watched to reassure himself that all was

well. ‘Bumph’, the gas ignited with a flash of multi-colours and the kettle went on.

Next morning when the lads had finished washing and arguing playfully amongst themselves, they all piled in for breakfast. There was no sign of their Dad’s presence.

“Where’s Dad, Mom?” asked Trevor.

“He’s gone for a little walk, just to see what he can see, he won’t be long.”

Mrs White had packed sufficient enough food to give them a start on this holiday. Holidays for them must start with a good breakfast, and this had been one of her main food priorities. So everyone had a plate with a fried egg, a rasher of bacon, a sausage and a heap of baked beans. There was a smell of toasting bread coming from the cooker grill. Mrs White pulled out the hot rack and took the toast off, ready to butter. Just at that moment, Frank poked his head through the door; he had a paper tucked under his left arm and a brown paper bag in his right hand.

“What’s that, Frank?” asked Floss.

Frank passed the bag over to her. It was full of bright red plums.

“Oh! They look good, don’t they?”

“That’s why I bought them. There’s a Co-Op just a few minutes’ walk down the lane, next to a post office.”

“A Co-Op, what they got there?”

“It’s well-stocked, just like ours; they got almost everything we’ll need. So we’ve got no need to panic.”

After they’d finished breakfast and a little later that morning, they left the carriages locked up and, after only a short wait they all clambered onto the local bus. At the front, above the driver, it read, ‘St Agnes’. It took them only a few stops and approximately ten to fifteen minutes to arrive there. The bus stopped directly outside of the St Agnes Head Hotel and opposite to what appeared to be large church buildings and gardens. As they stood there for just a few moments, getting their bearings, they saw that nuns were entering and leaving the gardens. Having never seen this occurrence before, they all watched with interest to see the nuns mingling with the morning shoppers, being greeted and leaving shops with their own goods. It was an unusual sight for their eyes amongst the local community along Fore Street. Frank suggested to them that the building must be a Convent. Floss wondered why they were not restricted in their movements as she had always believed this to be the case.

Mr White then suggested that they should find the seafront and return into the village later. So he stopped the first passer-by and asked directions. They set off down a slight incline, firstly down the lane and then zigzagging through trees on what became a very pretty walk. There were a few cottages along the way, and facing out onto the cove, which they could now see opening up before them. There was a large hotel-come-restaurant overlooking the beach on the right of the road. However, just before they got quite that far, the children had noticed that there was a bungalow on the left of the lane with a large pool in the gardens. It appeared to have lots of movement going on and there were a few other people stood by the wall overlooking it.

"God, what's that?" asked Josh.

It was something that they had only ever before seen in pictures but now here they were close at hand. They were seals; seals of differing size, and there were at least seven of them. There was a big wooden sign above the corner of the curving wall and Trevor read it out aloud, it said, 'St Agnes Seal Sanctuary'. There was a rectangular wooden moneybox attached to each of the wooden posts. These had the words written in white paint upon them, 'Kind

Donations'.

I can still today, after all these years having passed between, pull from a little slot within my memory bank, my memories of life upon that day. The sun was shining brilliantly and it was very warm; I remember seeing that small cove of St Agnes for the first time in my young life. It had upon the beach, a number of small, upturned fishing boats and, at the top line of the beach, there was a broad string of shale bordered by a small sloping random rock wall, just right for sitting upon. To the left-hand side of the cove there were some very strange and curious 'Oxo-cube' looking blocks, haphazardly piled to a great height, below the granite cliffs and disappearing snake-like into the pale blue, creamy foamed waters of the ocean. The breeze blew warmly and delicately across my pale skin, and the gulls, soaring in and out from beach to sea, squealed out their delight. There was a strong, salty-fishy-tarred smell that filled my nostrils and cleared my lungs. I just could not wait to sink my bare toes into that golden sand that ran invitingly downward just below the ribbon of pebbles that stretched the width of the cove. It was just at that moment as I was slipping off my sandals and struggling with my socks that Pearl noticed there was a small window to the one corner of the beachside restaurant from where they were selling ice-cream cones. I remember looking up as she squealed this out, and seeing a boy smaller than I was, with bright red hair and freckles, standing just in front of the window licking on the yellow Cornish ice cream. I had never seen such an ice cream before; this even outdid Mr Whippy. Dad bought cornets for everyone and we sat to eat them, along the stone wall, in a line, descending neatly in height order from Dad to me, all six of us. The ice cream was rich and creamy and its taste swam around my mouth, under my tongue and around my gums, never again since that day has the taste of an ice cream been so delicious has it was then.

We spent about two glorious hours there that first time upon St Agnes Cove beach, and then we retraced our steps back into the village, until, once more, we were all stood there outside of the St Agnes Hotel. Dad suggested that he'd go inside to enquire if children were allowed in the premises. He returned and told us that we would all be allowed through the lounge and out into the rear yard, where we were welcome to sit on the benches. I had never been inside such a large room; it had glass chandeliers, leather sofas and portraits hanging upon the walls. We passed from one entrance to the other and found ourselves in the garden where there were only a few benches and tables. I remember that a lot of the large, slabbed yard was taken up by a huge number of beer barrels. We tapped on some of them to find that mostly they were empty, all but a few. Dad said that they were waiting for the Draymen to make their collection. We kids sat upon a few of them while Dad went in to fetch some drinks but then we noticed that there were lots of wasps flying to and fro, in and out of the open plug holes upon the casks. We watched them and it appeared that they were taking in the remaining drops of the ale that lay there. All around the edge of the enclosed yard there were tall, frail-stemmed flowers; sort of wispy in appearance with dagger like leaves. I had seen leaves like this on flowers back at home, I believed that they were called Gladioli, but these leaves were small in comparison. The flowers were of differing shades, from the most vivid red, to paler orange in colour. They all swayed gently in the breeze whilst a variety of coloured butterflies flew in and out of them.

I remember Mom walking along the edge, stroking her hand through these and smelling their perfume. She remarked upon how wonderful they were and when Dad returned, she asked if he knew what they were, but he didn't. Dad had returned carrying a tray with six drinks upon it, but shortly after him, there followed a round-faced lady wearing a little black pinafore; she was carrying another tray with four Cornish pasties upon it. Dad and Mom had a pasty each but we kids shared the other two they were big ones. I had never tasted a pie as good as these at home. Half of one was plenty enough for Liam and I – they were big ones filled with large chunks of meat and vegetables – but Trevor did a bit of moaning about having to share one with Pearl. If I remember correctly, Dad said to Mom that his beer was called St Austell Ale. I asked, "St Austell, Dad, where's St Austell then?" He told me that it was somewhere up the coast but we were unlikely to see it. We had had a great day out on the beach and now Dad continued to tell his silly stories and jokes, pulling funny faces, and keeping us all laughing. How much I loved him, words cannot express. Liam was forever saying how funny my Dad was and throughout the holiday he wished that his Mom and Dad could be there enjoying it too. That first day in Cornwall was one of those days in your life that you keep locked up within a small treasure trove of memories that you occasionally withdraw to look upon admiringly.

The next morning, when I got up and went into the living carriage, Dad was missing again. Mom said that he had gone off on one of his early morning walks. He sometimes did this at home too; he always said that the early morning was the best time of the day. He was also probably missing the exercise of taking his early bike ride into work. He was later returning that morning, coming in when we were halfway through our breakfasts. He said that he had found the way into Chapel Porth and that it was an easy walk through the fields just across the lane – we didn't need to catch a bus. So right after breakfast had been cleared away, and the crocks washed, Dad started making sandwiches whilst Mom made tea and put it into our flasks. They packed towels and everything we needed for the day out into the bags, but outside the weather was nowhere near as fine as the day before. The wind had picked up a little and the sun dodged in and out of the clouds. We left the railway carriages at about 10.30am, and crossed the lane to climb over a wooden stile that had a finger post pointing and stating, 'Public Footpath'. We had to cross three fields in total. The first one had sheep grazing in it and the second Dad said was a field of turnips. I remember that we had to keep close into the hedge and walk in single file through that one. The third field unfortunately, well most unfortunately for Mom that is, had two horses in it. Mom did not like being so close to horses the only exception being that the racing rails of a racecourse should separate them. She loved her horseracing but had a fear that the horses might run at her. She initially refused to enter the field and moaned at Dad for not having warned her that there were horses in one of the fields that we had to cross. She took a lot of persuading before she entered that field and having trailed behind us through the previous fields, she led us hastily through this one, always giving the horses a wide berth. I remember that we had to stop for a while when we reached the far side and reached a narrow lane because Mom had to catch her breath.

To see Chapel Porth for the first time was just as dramatic and exciting as that first view of St Agnes was. This was a very similar cove; slightly smaller in its width but still having the high cliffs to either side, rearing up ruggedly out of the waters. Unlike St Agnes, it did not have the surrounding buildings. The entrance to the beach is elevated, causing you to look downwards out onto the sands once more across a shingle arc, but in this instance there are also rocks of varying proportions leading down onto the shingle. These rocks were very slippy and there was a strong wind blowing inward from the sea; strong enough to blow you about a bit. I said that this day's weather had started off poorly but everything here now seemed to be exaggerated. This was the roughest that I had ever seen a tide and still remains so. The narrowness of the cove may well have been the reason why the sea tides entered in here with such force. I know that I was small then but these waves seemed as high as double-decker buses. They entered the cove and grew both in momentum and size roaring deafeningly as they did so. For the first time ever I saw surfers riding the waves. It was difficult to grasp why they were not being battered and bruised by the sheer force. We all stood and watched in admiration the strength and determination of these distant figures being lifted, rolled, and thrown high upwards into the air then falling downwardly into the gaping chasm were once the waters where. Perseverance was certainly their middle names. Dad was just suggesting that we should find a sheltered spot between the sand dunes when we heard voices from behind us. I suppose because of the quiet isolation of this cove we were surprised, and we all turned around to look at who was approaching at the same instant. We saw a young couple; the lady was carrying a baby wrapped in a woollen shawl, the man led the way but was looking around, holding out a hand, because she seemed to be struggling across the slippery rocks. Suddenly, she slipped and instinctively she threw the baby outwards onto the shale in front of them. It was horrific to witness this, and all of us feared for the safety of the baby. The lady fell very awkwardly and heavily amongst the large boulders and lay screaming in pain. The man, who I presumed to be her husband, moved quickly to her aid. Mom and Dad both rushed forward to help. Mom instinctively went straight for the baby being concerned that it must have been badly hurt. It must have been a real dilemma for the man being faced with such a choice as to who he should help first. Dad went to both the man and the lady's side. He helped the man to lift the lady upwards into a sitting position but it was obvious from the shouting that she had caused some real harm to herself.

I went over towards Mom. She was now cradling the small baby in her arms and miraculously, whether it was the cushioning of the blanket in which it was wrapped, who can say, but the baby seemed completely unharmed just shaken up by the experience. Mom soon quietened it down; she had had plenty of experience with children. We took the baby over to the lady's side. She appeared to be in a lot of pain but was frantic about the baby's welfare. She kept repeating a girl's name; I think it was Brenda. Mom quickly reassured her that all was well and she held the baby closely to the lady but she was in too much discomfort to move. She simply nodded and thanked us. Dad and Trevor had disappeared and the man told us that Dad had been certain that he had not long since seen a telephone kiosk out on the lane and that's where they had gone. The lady's head was bleeding badly and her partner had wrapped a towel around it, which was rapidly becoming bloodstained. Her ankle was also cut and was swelling into a balloon; the man feared that she had broken it. Mom told the lady that her actions had most likely saved the girl from injury. The little girl continued to cry but no worse than any other child of that age. Trevor and Dad were a little while returning to us and it must have only been a few minutes later that we could hear the whine of the ambulance siren. The ambulance men soon had the lady up onto a stretcher, and both Dad and her partner steadied them across the rocks to safety. The man shouted his thanks to us from the rear door of the ambulance just as they were being closed. We all returned, with greater care than previously, back out onto the beach. We found our little protected place within the dunes but this day had been soured for us. Mom couldn't forget the state of the lady and the concern that she had first had for the child. She kept wondering how they were and how badly the lady had been hurt.

Later that same afternoon, shortly after we had returned to our holiday carriage, it started to rain, so we were unable to leave that evening. We had to make do with playing games of cards, dominoes and eye-spy. The wind throughout that day had gradually strengthened and the train carriages had begun to shake and rattle upon the tracks. By the time we had got into our beds you could hear the wind howling through the trees along the lane. The following morning when I awoke I was still greeted by the same howling wind. I pulled aside the little window curtain to see that the rain had stopped but the day's weather still appeared to hold no promise of improvement. When Liam and I went through to the kitchen we found Mom and Pearl already preparing breakfast but Dad had gone off on his regular morning stroll. Mom was very concerned about him but he had insisted that a little bit of wind would cause him no harm. When he had still not returned, and the breakfast things were being cleared away, we were all concerned. This was unlike Dad; he had an uncanny knack of being there just in time for his meals. Trevor suggested to Mom that he should go out and look for him but Mom wasn't too sure, but she grew more impatient as we waited for him and time passed by. Eventually she agreed that it would be alright for Trevor to go, and Liam and I begged her to let us go too. Pearl would stay to keep Mom company until we returned. When we arrived out onto the lane we had no idea which way we should go and were under strict instructions not to split up. Trevor suggested that we should turn right down the lane, and head in the direction of the Post Office. I remember asking, how about if he had crossed the fields again, but Trevor was insistent that we must choose one way and that it was best that we stayed along the lanes.

All the while we walked there was a constant howling of the wind. It was as if something unnatural was trying to make contact. I know that this seems a little stupid in retrospect but it was probably one of, if not, the most eerie experiences of my lifetime. We were walking down the right hand side of the lane alongside the hawthorne hedging and tall trees. It wasn't that far to the Post Office but there was nothing between us and it along the lane. The Post Office wasn't in view because the lane veered firstly to the left and then back towards the right. There was no traffic at all along the lane and not a single person passed us by. The continual blustering wind blew us about and the trees rustled and moaned. It was just before the Post Office came into view, close to a request bus stop on our side of the lane, that I, and I think Trevor, must have noticed at exactly the same moment in time, that there were a lot of newspapers, soaking wet and draped over and across the bench that stood opposite. We all crossed the lane, I don't know why, but it surely must have been instinctively, towards the bench. It hadn't rained since we had got up earlier that morning and I don't know at what time it had ceased, so how long must the papers have been there? I remember having this awful feeling; I didn't like it. It was the most awful feeling that I had ever had in my lifetime. The wind was still blowing, first with whispers and then with tormented screeches as if it tried to speak to us. It was a very lonely place and we were just three scared young children. Scared of what, I don't know probably the unknown but at the time it was scary. Trevor approached the bench in front of Liam and I, and has he went to touch the paper I remember saying, “Leave it Trevor, leave it!”

Then I was startled out of my wits as I heard the voice of a woman shouting, “Wait!”

I looked up to see that it was the lady who we had all seen the day before in the Post Office. Trevor had stopped dead in his tracks. She came over towards us and suggested that we should move away. I didn’t understand, but Trevor moved towards us and pulled us both together into his arms. What were we so frightened of and why had the lady asked us to move away? I was terrified as she carefully approached the sodden papers and, standing between the object and us, she began to peel back one corner of the newspapers. We were close enough to see a pair of battered old shoes being revealed. I suddenly thought about Dad, where was he? The lady moved to the other end of the bench and again repeated her movements. This time with even greater care, and probably with much anxiety, she turned back just a small corner, half revealing a face. My heart was in my mouth; I don’t know how the others felt. I couldn’t see properly and I didn’t know if the others could or not. My throat restricted; then she lowered the paper and came over to us. She asked what we were doing there. Trevor explained to her about Dad and she said that she had seen him just ten minutes earlier. Thank God. This was not Dad. Then who was it? The lady began to explain to us about a local tramp that slept nightly upon this same bench for many years. A lot of the locals had tried to be of assistance to him but he never accepted their offers. She appeared to have a tear in her eye and obviously thought kindly of him. “He must have passed away quietly in his sleep,” she said. She asked if we might kindly stay with him whilst she went and telephoned for help. Trevor agreed, so we stood there for a short while in that desolated place of death.

Trevor took us directly back to our rail carriages and all I could think of on that short journey was what I had seen and that poor lonely man. When we opened the carriage door Dad was stood there, he had arrived shortly in front of us. He said that he was about to come straight back out and look for us. I noticed immediately that his thumb and forefinger were bleeding.

"What's happened to you Dad?" I asked, taking hold of his hand.

"Oh, it's nothing!" he said, and he patted me upon the head with his free hand. "Where have you lot been then?" he asked.

Trevor said, "We've just seen something really horrible, Dad."

We were, by now, all taking off our coats and I looked at Dad's hand again and asked, "How did you do that, Dad?"

He replied, "Oh, I just slipped on a damp stone and put my arm out to stop myself, it's nothing son, now Trevor tell me what you lot have seen that was so horrible?"

Trevor continued, "It was horrible…"

Just then Mom appeared from out of one of the bedrooms.

"What was horrible?" she asked.

Trevor got annoyed, "I'm trying to tell yer, ain't I!" He was irritated.

Cutting the story very short, he shouted out, "This tramp was dead on a bench!"

"What tramp?" Dad asked.

I butted in, "Some tramp that sleeps regularly on a bench along the lane, opposite the bus stop close to the Post Office."

Trevor enquired, "Didn't you see him Dad?"

"No!" he replied. "But I crossed the land opposite the Post Office and came back through the woods." Holding his injured hand up, he said, "That's where I did this."

Mom jumped up immediately and said with concern, "Oh Frank, let me take a look at that, you shouldn't be sitting there talking with blood dripping from your hand."

When Mom held up Dad's hand by the wrist she noticed that his wristwatch had been smashed. "Look at yer watch Frank."

"Blimey!" he said. "I never saw that."

Dad's watch was ruined. The glass was smashed and it didn't matter what he did to try and restart it, it just would not go.

The following morning we all caught the bus right after breakfast to go down to Penzance. Dad told us that Penzance was like London was to England – the capital city of Cornwall, a really big place. I shall never forget the first sight I had of it as we arrived on the bus. Well, in fact, we hadn't quite arrived, because the first thing that we set eyes on, from a distance, on the approach, were two huge gas cylinders; the type of things that rise and fall with the volume of gas. Most of the towns of the Black Country are dotted with these, and you don't expect the beauty of a seaside resort to be spoiled by them. However, I was soon aware that first sight judgements are not always correct. Beyond these cylinders, the town of Penzance and the harbour are indeed very beautiful. It is also very large compared to everywhere that we'd seen up until this time. We spent some time viewing the harbour, watching the fishermen at work and admiring the various boats. The weather was like it had been on the first day in St Agnes; warm and sunny. We sat outside a couple of pubs as we investigated the harbour, right opposite the sea, looking out upon the distant horizon. We ate more pasties and then we went into a shop to get some Cornish fudge; we took it over to the harbour wall and sat with our legs dangling above the sea, making pigs of ourselves.

Mom wanted to have a look around the shops, for some reason, like most women do. So at around 3.00pm we were walking up and down Fore Street. The one side of the road here is set up above the other by three or four steps, like a raised pavement, and very unusual. We were stood looking inside a shop that sold model replica sailing ships; some very large and designed with a great amount of detail in them. Dad was pointing out one or two of the better known ones, well better known to him that is, like the Hispaniola, the Santa Rosa and the Mayflower. When we finally looked up to move on, Pearl and Mom were missing. Dad said that he had never seen them leave and neither did we. We decided that it was best to wait where we were for a few minutes but then we noticed that Mom was just leaving a jewellers shop a few doors on. Dad asked, "Where have you been, we thought we had lost you?"

Mom had a little bag in her hand and Pearl was pestering her for it. Mom passed it to her and she handed it to Dad. Dad opened it very carefully; inside was a small black box, which he took out. He opened the box carefully not knowing what to expect; he pulled out a silver pocket watch. We all wanted to look at it but he said,

"Hold yer horses, let me see it first."

He turned it about, meticulously examining it and on the back he found an engraving. He read it and then he took Mom by the shoulder and kissed her.

"It's handsome," he said "Thank you."

I got it after Trevor, and it was handsome. I loved it, the engraving was a small heart with the letters F.W. clearly marked. F.W. was in fact both Dad's and Mom's initials.

That week in Cornwall passed by far too quickly. There

had been some misfortune during it and the memory of the lady throwing her baby into the air to save it from worse injury, then finding the dead tramp on that awful morning; I knew that that would live with me for the rest of my life, but so would the happiness, the love and those wonderful sights. I believe that there were a few tears on that Saturday morning as we finished filling our bags to return home. Liam whispered to me, "I wish this could have lasted forever." The train journey home was far less enjoyable than the one going there. Dad was back at work on the Monday morning and a return to school was looming ever nearer.

CHAPTER FOUR

Two Months Later

(THE DECLINE BEGINS)

On the Saturday afternoon Dad took us to the Baggies; me, Trevor and Liam. I remember them beating Q.P.R. 5-1. Mom and Pearl had gone into Birmingham, shopping for the day. That night we all met down at the pub, and sat outside in the gardens; Liam's Mom and Dad came with us. I remember Mr Hullstone talking to Dad about the holiday that they had all agreed that we should go on together the following year. Mrs Hullstone kept saying, "Our Liam never shuts up about it." It will be brilliant, I thought, all of us, it will be better for Liam to have his Mom and Dad there. They had agreed that we should go right at the very beginning of the next summer holidays and it was something that they were all really looking forward to. Dad said that we kids should all save our pocket money so that we would be well financed for it. The conversation then changed as Liam told me that he and his Dad were going fishing the following day. Mr Hullstone said that if I wanted to, I could go with them, but me, Dad and Trevor had already planned to go off on our bikes, so I said, "no thank you." Liam loved his fishing but I'm afraid that I found it a little bit too boring so I didn't go very often with them.

At 10.00am on the Sunday morning the three of us set off together heading for Sutton Park. Dad had asked Trevor to take the lead and he'd be tail-end, just so that he could keep a watchful eye over the pair of us. We took it steady;

the weather was still excellent especially for late October – very fresh and warm. There was very little traffic on the roads and when we arrived at Sutton Park we found it was really quiet; Sundays usually drew a few more visitors in. I remember most of all, the wonderful colours of the leaves on the trees; deep reds, purples, yellows and a few remaining green ones, defiant of the oncoming winter. This year had been an exceptionally dry one, and the grass in the park was a little threadbare and brown in patches. We rode straight onwards through the park until we arrived at the lakeside. It was then that we dismounted and stood the bikes together beside a huge Oak before sitting down beside the water. There was a large pair of swans just casually drifting by. The water was like a giant tinted mirror with shades of green, grey and black. The swan's reflections made them appear double-decker; so graceful and majestic, they moved without effort; beautiful birds with silky, snowy feathers. I remember that Dad had brought orange juice along with us but he surprised us too by pulling out of his rucksack a wagon wheel for each of us, although Mom's last words had been to watch what we had so as not to spoil our lunches. We must have stayed for about forty-five minutes, had a ride around the park (Trevor and I had a race, he won as always), then we returned home in the same order as we had arrived in.

Dad said that he would be working late the following night and that we should behave for Mom. I knew that when he worked late, he sometimes stopped off at the pub on the way home "for a quick pint," as he put it. Sometimes we were in bed before he returned. On weekday nights we were never allowed to stop up late and we always had to do our homework before we went to bed. That weekend had been a good weekend. There were many good weekends. For a family with little money we were happy, very happy. You can be happy with just sufficient to get you through as long as life is good. I loved my Mom and Dad very dearly and I'm sure that they loved me. Trevor wasn't that bad as big brothers go and Pearl, well, Pearl was a girl after all, but she was okay I suppose.

Monday morning of that week was a normal morning as normal as any other Monday morning. A little hectic but that's normal. Dad had gone before I had got up and Mom was rushing about, Trevor wouldn't get out of bed and Pearl had lost her P.E. kit. I had toast and jam for breakfast and Mom kept pushing my fringe back with her wet fingers and saying, "Why doesn't your hair behave itself?" Trevor finally dragged himself out of bed and joined us and Mom pointed to Pearl's kit in the corner of the kitchen, ready waiting for her. Trevor ate hardly anything, swigged back his juice and was still tying his red school tie as he rushed through the door. Me, Pearl and Mom followed less than five minutes later. She dropped us off at school and then, as she did usually, went on to do her weekly shopping; a normal Monday.

Mom picked us up from school in the afternoon, me and Pearl, that is. Trevor, she said, had already dashed in and out again before she had left home, saying that he was off to play football with his mates. I remember she took us into town, because she had forgotten a few things, and we ended up having a walk around the Art Gallery. We went on to have fish and chips. We must have arrived home at about six o'clock. Liam phoned me and asked what we had been doing because he had been trying to call me. He was going fishing with his Dad again, just on the canal but they had had to put it off because their washing machine had sprung a leak. He said that his Dad was up to his ankles in water. I played out in the garden for a while and Mom sat at the kitchen table with Pearl working on some difficult science homework. Pearl was not very scientific. Being eleven now, Pearl had much more homework than I did. I rarely had any. Later we all watched Coronation Street together; I remember that it was the episode when the funeral of Martha Longhurst occurred, and Trevor said jokingly, as the cars pulled into the cemetery, "Here comes Martha's long-hearse." Mom laughed until she almost fell off her chair, the rest of the country was probably in tears. Strangely enough I can't remember much at all after that. Someone knocked on our door and I jumped up to answer it

At the front door I remember pausing for a second; I felt a little strange inexplicable. I opened the door slowly, we weren't expecting any visitors. There were two uniformed officers standing before me; a man and a young woman. It was dark outside; the street light across the road from us divided one officer from the other. The policeman asked, "Is your Mom in, son?"

I hesitated and then replied, "Yes."

"Can we come in then, please?"

I remember instinctively calling out for Mom because I didn't know if I was doing the right thing letting strangers into the house. Mom came to the middle door calling out, "What is it, Josh?"

I was halfway turned about. Mom stepped into the hallway and saw the police. I still remember how the colour drained from her face; she looked white and shocked. She started mumbling, "Oh no, oh no!"

I didn't understand but immediately the police lady moved towards her and supported her. I don't know why but I started to cry. It's difficult to explain because I had no idea what was going on. We all walked into the living room and Pearl jumped up to help Mom when she saw her. She kept asking, "What is it Mom? What's happened?"

Nothing had been said and neither of us really

understood but I knew that Mom did and I knew that it was something bad. Mom told us to sit down and then she invited the police officers to sit too; the tears ran down her face and I didn't know why. Pearl comforted her and Trevor went to put the kettle on. The policeman asked, "Is it alright with the children here?"

Mom just nodded and said, "Tell me, just tell me."

I sat on the arm of the chair by her side and clutched at her arm.

The policeman asked, "Are you Florence White?"

Mom replied, "Yes."

"And is your husband Frank White?"

Again she said, "Yes."

He asked Mom if there was anyone who could look after us because he needed her to accompany them to the station. 'With them, why should Mom go with them?' I thought. I was still crying. Trevor gave Mom a cup of tea and asked if the officers wanted one, they replied, "No thank you."

Mom said that Mrs Talbot next-door, she pointed towards the direction, would probably come around and sit with us. The policewoman got up from her seat and left the house. She returned within minutes with Mrs Talbot at her side. She just grabbed Mom and they both cried together; I cried even more to see them so distressed but I still didn't understand.

A week to that day, on the following Monday, at 3.00pm, the funeral service was held at St Francis Xavier. My Dad was dead, killed, they said, by a hit and run driver as he left the Tiger Public House on his bicycle. People were saying all sorts of things; that "He had been drunk," and that, "He was probably to blame anyway." It was awful. Whenever I saw Mom she was crying. I cried too, and so did Trevor and Pearl. I had never cried so much in my life, and this was the first funeral that I had ever had to attend. My own Dad's funeral; I just could not believe that he would never be coming home again. That he'd never throw me over his shoulder once more; never hang me upside down, and never take us on another bicycle ride or holiday. The night that it had happened we were up until the early hours and I don't think Mom ever got into her bed at all. All of that week we were kept off school and all that I can remember was that I constantly sat by the front window, day after day, just looking for him, hoping and wishing, but he never came, he never came again.

We had several visits from the police. Sometimes I was sent out of the room but at others I stayed and I heard the things that were said. I also heard several of the neighbours talking; friends and relatives, some I hadn't seen for years. I heard them say that he wasn't drunk. I heard them say that the gaffer at the Tiger had said that he had never, ever seen my Dad drunk. Witnesses all said that when my Dad had left the pub, a dark blue saloon car, being driven by a man, had swung sharply around the bend and ploughed straight through him, just as he left the car park. Apparently the car never swerved or braked; they all said that it never even slowed down but just continued on down the road with the driver not even glancing backwards. Not one of them got the registration number; they all said that it happened so quickly. Dad's boss from his work came to see Mom and he told her that, Dad "had not clocked off until 6.45pm." That meant, I remember Mom saying, that the journey on his bike to the pub would have taken about fifteen minutes and that if as everyone had said the accident occurred at about 7.40pm; then Dad could have only been in the pub for approximately thirty-five minutes. She phoned the Gaffer afterwards at the Tiger and he agreed with her that those times would have been about right. He said that it was difficult to remember exactly, because it had been a busy time, but he assured Mom that Dad had drunk just two pints and no more. He had shouted goodnight as he had left and that was it.

At school some of the kids became obnoxious; taunting me, saying that my Dad was a drunkard and that he couldn't ride a bike. They said that their Moms had said that he should have been at home with his wife and kids. That was when the first real fights of my life began; I wasn't having it. It was bad at home with Trevor having gone real quiet and spending loads of time either locked up in his bedroom or away from the house. Pearl was all over Mom and I felt isolated, choked, my head was buzzing and I often felt sick. I no longer wanted to go to school but Mom always said it was for the best. I couldn't tell her about what was happening and I knew that Trevor had started wagging it regularly. He probably had the same problems I had but we didn't talk. It wasn't long before Mom started to get calls from the schools, telling her about both of us. Trevor's headmaster said that although they could well understand the tragic circumstances, it was still not good enough. Mom told me to stop fighting and to think what Dad would have thought of me. She didn't know that it was because of Dad that I was fighting.

Liam and his Mom and Dad called around regularly. They were a big help to Mom. I think that it was them who told Mom what a lot of the fights at school were about, and that Liam was also becoming involved. Whenever he had overheard anyone bad-mouthing Dad, he was just as bad as me. I know that Liam had also loved my Dad but no one could ever have loved him as much as I did. Some people brought Mom pies and stuff. Pies didn't replace Dad. Mom said that it was good of them but I sometimes got angry. Pearl sometimes slept with Mom to keep her company but I slept on my own, it seemed as if there was no one for me. Trevor always turned nasty should I ever attempt to speak Dad's name. He was full of anger and, just as I did, he came home on several occasions with black eyes, cut lips and ripped clothing. I wanted us to become closer; I wanted us to be brothers, to support Mother and Pearl and when I think back now, I probably needed him to replace Dad. It just didn't happen. Trevor blamed everyone; I think that he blamed the world. He swore to me more than once that he would find out eventually who that driver had been and when he did he would kill him.

The police kept making promises to Mom that they would eventually arrest someone and that that 'someone' would be brought to justice. The local newspapers kept repeating the same thing and every so often Central News would have a report update; but time went on and on and the police visits became less frequent until eventually they petered out. I remember Trevor throwing something at the television on the one occasion that they were talking about it. He and Mom had a big row over his behaviour and the fact that it made nothing any better. Trevor ran out of the room shouting and slamming every door behind him. Mom was again left in tears. The next time the police called it was about Trevor; they said that they had caught him loosing the tyres down on a dark blue saloon car and then discovered that he had also been around the town doing this to several others. I was more annoyed because of the distress it caused to Mom. She was upset enough; we all had our troubles, and I now thought that Trevor was making it worse for the lot of us. Fortunately the police let Trevor off with a caution but it wasn't to be long before they were back again. Mom said that she was reaching the end of her tether, whatever that meant, but she just didn't know what to do with him. Again the police, who were aware of the recent tragic circumstances, decided to just caution Trevor and did not press any charges.

I remember that I became very, very angry with Trevor following this last police visit. I called him a 'selfish git' and I followed him to his bedroom, where he would always go to hide himself away. He tried to slam the door in my face but I fought with him and the door to keep it from closing. Trevor caught my fingers in the door, it was nothing really but at that moment it made me erupt. I launched myself at him and threw things about in his room. He grabbed at me several times scratching my arms until finally he had a firm grip and managed to wrestle me down to the floor. There he managed to hold me by sitting upon my back until I almost couldn't breathe. I cried with anger and frustration, hatred and self pity. I cried for Mom and I cried for Dad. Eventually Trevor released me but without speaking a single word, he pushed me from his room and then locked the door. I just sat there on the landing, thinking to myself, 'he's my brother; I love him, why can't he love me too?' Half the time he couldn't even look at me, let alone try to talk to me; it seemed that he hated me. He hated us all because of Dad's death and he certainly knew how to punish us.

Trevor had his way of dealing with this situation in life and we all had ours. Instead of coming together with others who suffered the same loss, he chose to deal with it individually and privately. I was the youngest and there was still a lot about life that I had to learn. Trevor could have been my mentor, my crutch and my best friend but instead his hatred closed us all out. He rarely moved about the house amongst us. We could hear him come and go. Never again did he sit at the table for a meal. Mom had no answer so she gave in to it and soon it became natural. Mom had still not lifted herself from her own gloom, sadness and disconnection from life. Trevor hung around the streets and parks. He soon got involved with the wrong crowd. Occasionally he would bring some of them home with him and then things started to go missing from our house. Mom had money stolen from her purse. I remember that Mom even asked one day if I had taken money from her. It was very hurtful to think that Mom could even mistrust me. How could she ever believe that I would steal from her? Trevor sometimes brought a girl home and not always the same girl, in fact very rarely. He was still young and this time Mom could not ignore it. She told him that it had to stop and confronted him time and again. She occasionally escorted girls from the house. Trevor just ignored Mom and eventually and gradually, she did not tackle him, she gave in. As for Trevor and I, well I believe that this was when I realised that I had lost both a brother and a father. The day he threw me from his bedroom had been bad enough but now I totally disrespected him.

Liam was my best friend through all of this. I gradually sorted myself out with Liam and his parents' help. He became my brother and I loved him as my family. I also felt the need to be there for Mom and Pearl; I saw myself as their protector, but I was just a kid. Liam wanted me to do more and more stuff with him but I couldn't. I was needed at home. I think he understood but he was sometimes a little angry with me. He made no other friends, so he relied on me. At school it was different, of course we both had more mates but once we left school we had each other and our families. He really loved his fishing and he went with either his Dad or his Uncles, he always asked me to go but fishing wasn't my thing and I made excuses just to be at home.

At first the time passed very slowly and painfully but gradually we just fell into a routine. Pearl was very clingy around Mother. She was now twelve and, like me, hadn't got a group of friends; she didn't even have a regular pal to call upon her and to pass the time away with. So she helped Mom with the cooking, ironing and housework. Pearl was becoming old too early in life. Pearl and I were good friends but, after all, she was a girl and I was a boy; we liked different things. Pearl was developing differently to me and she was also putting on weight. She sat about for far too long with Mom and they were forever eating cakes. They cooked them, so they ate them. I liked cakes too but I also did the gardening and the errands. They had no interest whatsoever in gardening. I did it because Dad loved his garden and I couldn't see it fall into a wasteland. Even at this young age I was becoming very knowledgeable about plants and stuff although I struggled with the Latin names. I had always loved nature and what I missed most was our cycle rides to Sutton Park. Dad used to tell me everything and he would stop and point things out, he was always very enthusiastic about the simplest of natural things and I suppose it rubbed off on me. The bikes lay in the shed covered in an old sheet and dust. They were probably going rusty but I couldn't bring myself to look. As for the Baggies; well Mr Hullstone was never a really big supporter but he would occasionally, well very occasionally that is, take me and Liam to a match, mainly when it was kids for a quid.

The first twelve months that went by after Dad's death was very hard work for us all. Mom had to be very strong in order to look after the three of us. It must have been very difficult but somehow she got by. I know that Mrs Hullstone was a strong support for her early on but as time went on, well, Mrs Hullstone had her life and family to look after and we had ours. Trevor was no real help to any of us. He still expected his meals to be on the table and he shouted a lot about anything; especially if his clothes weren't ready when he wanted them. He was a pain in the butt!

Mom was forever getting bad reports from school about him and his behaviour. The neighbours did their share of moaning about his nuisance too and the Police called occasionally. Mom eventually found the strength to ban his worst friends from the house but that just meant that he went elsewhere to be with them. By now he had brought a string of girls home. He always took them to his bedroom and Mom found it easier not to discuss this at all. He was only fifteen. Mrs Hullstone told Mom that it just was not right and, on one occasion Mr Hullstone got very angry and he spoke with Trevor; he was trying to be helpful and to show Trev the upset he was causing but all he got was a mouthful of abuse for his efforts.

Mom had to start a new job because the money coming in was insufficient. She worked at the local Co-Op but had to arrange her hours around us lot. I remember it caused quite a bit of friction at times, especially with her boss, but we managed. Sometimes the neighbours next-door to us would be there when I came out of school and they would look after Pearl and me until Mom got back home. Mom never left us at night time though, well that is until about six months after Dad died and then, on the one Friday night, Mrs Gould came and looked after us. Mom must have returned home at about ten o'clock. I lay awake until I heard her talking with Mrs Gould. After the first time, this happened now and again but Mrs Gould said that Mom worked hard for us and deserved a bit of leisure time. Pearl would sometimes cry about it and I remember asking Mom why she had to go.

CHAPTER FIVE
Jack Shipley

The first time I ever saw him he was sitting in the kitchen at the table. I had just got back home with Mr Hullstone and Liam; we'd been to the swimming baths. It was very strange because Liam and his Dad would always stop for a cup of tea with Mom before they left, but on this occasion Mr Hullstone just nodded a swift hello and said, "Come on Liam, we have to go."

I followed them back up the hall to the door; the hall that we had only just walked up a few seconds before. I remember feeling a little odd about it all, and uncomfortable. I had no idea who this man was but I had felt an instant dislike for him. I went back in and Mom said that Pearl was around next-door with Mrs Gould; I didn't know if she was suggesting that I should go too. She then asked me to say hello to the man; she said that his name was 'Mr Shipley'. He rubbed my hair up and said, "Hello, son." I told Mom that I was going out to play in the garden. For some unknown reason I had taken a huge disliking to this man who was sat drinking tea in our kitchen with our Mother. Who was he and what was he doing here?

I was kicking the ball hard against the wall and Pearl must have heard me. She shouted over, "Is that you Josh?" and I answered her.

She then shouted "I'm coming back now."

She was back around with me in what seemed liked seconds. The first thing I asked her was, "Who's he?" Pearl said that she really didn't know but that he had arrived an hour earlier and Mom had simply just taken her immediately to Mrs Goulds. I said, "I don't like him, do you?"

"Josh we don't even know the man, be fair!"

"What do you mean, be fair?"

"Well, you can't judge people when you've only just met them, can you?

"There's something about him, I don't like him!" I replied.

This man, Shipley, was a short man, perhaps 5" 6" tall, but he was very broad, square-shouldered. He had slick black hair; it looked as if it was heavily Brylcreamed. He had a sort of long pointy nose and narrow eyes that were very dark in colour. He was smartly dressed with a suit and tie on. As I kicked the ball I remember watching him carefully all the time. His greasy hair seemed to have a habit of falling forward across his eyes at times, in strands. He just brushed it to one side. Who did he look like? Then I remembered; World War Two, we had done this at school. This man looked like Adolph Hitler. I realised that this must have been what had registered with me immediately, and that was probably the reason that I had taken the instant disliking to him.

I remember that day, after he had gone; Pearl and I asked Mom who he was, but all she would tell us was that he was an old friend of the family and that he had worked with Dad at one time. We pressed her but she would say no more, only that his first name was Jack. I told her straight that I didn't like him and that he looked like Hitler; I remember her just giving a little chuckle and dismissing me with, "Don't be silly Josh." I hoped that we never saw him again but we hadn't seen the last of Jack Shipley. There were more occasions when I returned home to find him sitting upon the same kitchen chair. After these visits, the times that Mom left us with Mrs Gould began to increase. I only protested less when I started to realise that Mom's old smile seemed to be returning, slowly and gradually she was becoming my Mom again. She smiled and joked with us like she had before we lost Dad and I tried to be happy for her. It seemed to take a very long time for Jack Shipley to become any sort of an established figure in our house but he popped up on all sorts of occasions and gradually he was there. Trevor did not like him and he did not notice Mom's returning happiness. He refused to speak to him. I thought that my indifference was bad enough – I still did not like him – but Trevor refused even to acknowledge him.

Trevor was still being Trevor; I longed to have a brother back, we needed one another so much. Or was it just me who needed him? I preferred to believe that we needed each other and I persevered in trying to re-establish our relationship. Trevor tended to shun me. There was however one occasion, when I had arrived back home all teary after school because one of the elder lads had pushed me about. I was sat in the kitchen pouring my heart out to Mom, telling her all about it, and I was aware that Trevor was sitting just outside on the garden wall. I knew that he must have been able to hear what I was saying; but he never came in and said a word. But just after I remember him dashing out brushing past Mom on the way; I heard the door slam. This sort of behaviour was really not exceptional for Trevor. It wasn't until the following day at school, when I saw my previous day's tormentor sporting a black eye, that I began to wonder. It was a real shiner and better still, he avoided me completely. He gave me a real wide berth and never bothered me that day; in fact he never bothered me again. Some of my friends later told me that the school grapevine was saying that Trevor had caught him playing in the park that evening and that he had really laid into him. I tried to speak to Trevor about it on several occasions but he was his normal self and just kept the distance between us. The day after I had heard this rumour, I spent my tuck money on sweets from the corner shop, and when I got home I just placed them in Trevor's room. Normally he would have gone off like a rocket knowing that I had been into his room but he never said a word.

Trevor behaved exactly the same towards Pearl as he did with me but Pearl did not try so hard to re-establish the relationship. She was content with hanging out with Mom but she and I always did little things together too. Liam hadn't known about what happened that day I had been bullied at school; when he did find out he said that he would have helped me had he known. I knew that he was just acting bravely and I wouldn't have wanted him to get hurt too. Strange thing was that when I spoke to him about Trevor and his general behaviour, well he couldn't understand. He told me that there had been many occasions when he and his Dad had been fishing on the canal side and Trev had come along; he added that Trevor always stopped to talk to them. I said that Trev and his Dad had once had a bit of a row about girls at home, but Liam told me that Trevor had since apologised to Mr Hullstone, and that they got on really well and always had done. Then Liam said that his Dad and Trevor had once had a discussion about Jack Shipley whilst they sat fishing, and neither of them liked him. Mr Hullstone had never really spoken to me about Jack but I was pleased that he disliked him too. Apparently Liam's Dad had said that Jack used to work with Dad at his old works and that lots of the men there reckoned that they had never seen eye to eye. Dad wasn't a nasty person and I knew that he had loads of friends so this was unusual. Mr Hullstone also reckoned that rumour had it that there had been blows struck between them on more than one occasion. When I returned home I tried to talk to Mom about this; asking her if she had been aware of this ill feeling but she just told me not to be silly. She said that it was probably all a load of rubbish. I couldn't believe that she would dismiss it like that. I remember saying that I didn't think Mr Hullstone would say it if it was, and that he didn't talk rubbish. Mom was having none of it.

Jack Shipley kept arriving at our house whenever he liked, or he was already there making himself comfortable when I got there. It was all getting very cosy and my hatred grew following Liam's revelations. It had been good to see Mom happy and joking again but it now, again, felt all wrong. She was always dressing up; wearing things that I had never seen her in before. I very often thought that she looked too young for her age. I'd heard Mom use the expression, 'mutton dressed as lamb', or something to that effect. This was now how I was beginning to look at my own Mother. I just didn't like to tell her to upset her. Sometimes she would ask my opinion, saying, "How does this look on me?" or "Does this fit properly at the rear?" Pearl always buttered her up so I tried to make her feel good too. Shipley tried to start conversations with me by asking, how I'd done at school on a particular day, or had I been playing football, etc. I always tried to answer him in one word if I could. I just could not bring myself to like him. He seemed false. He had a crooked smile and seemed absolutely full of himself. The one day he told us that he had won some monies, 'on the gee-gees' – his words not mine – he pushed a five pound note into my hands and I immediately told him that I didn't want it. (It was probably the first fiver I'd ever held and had it not been his I'd have accepted it gladly). Mom gave me a look when I pushed it back at him. He gave it to her and told her to get me something nice. I didn't want his money or him; I didn't want to owe him a thing. I went up to my room and fetched Dad's photo out of the top drawer of my cupboard. I wanted Dad back; nothing else mattered to me.

Mom had regular nights out now, and Jack Shipley gave Mrs Gould something for looking after us. Sometimes I'd just lie awake in bed listening for the sound of Mom's voice. I wanted so much for her to be my old Mom but then I'd hear the sound of Shipley's voice as well. They'd be laughing and joking until the early hours of the morning and I hated it. I knew that she must be drinking more now than I had ever seen her drink before. She spoke with a high pitch and giggled a lot when she'd had too much. This behaviour annoyed me a lot. Trevor very often stopped at his mates' houses and he made no attempt whatsoever to talk to Shipley. He didn't talk to me much; in fact he spoke little of anything around the house but he made it so obvious that he was avoiding Shipley. We shared this mutual dislike but Trevor refused to discuss it with me. The most I ever got was, "It's Mom's life now, not ours!" Pearl and I drew closer, if anything, because of Shipley. She didn't share our hatred for him; at least if she did she didn't acknowledge it. However, she did start to recognise the change in Mom's behaviour and the times that we were being 'dumped!' (Not too nice a word, is it? But this is how it seemed). Mom was neglecting us. Pearl missed the close relationship that had developed so intensely between them following Dad's death. Don't misunderstand me; Mom wasn't neglecting our well-being, our food and our clothes. She gave us our pocket-money and we all knew that she loved us, but, when she was with him, nothing else seemed to matter. Pearl never ever now shared Mom's bed. Pearl started to become more independent. Another change at home was the lack of visits from old friends or relations. The Hullstones very rarely popped by, and Mr Hullstone would drop me off but never come in for a cuppa. I either went to see Liam at his house or we would be going out somewhere together. Pearl started to kick the ball about with me in the garden, either because she enjoyed it or didn't want to be inside. She regularly helped me with my homework as well; Mom never did now, and there was no one else to ask.

I remember the one day I returned home and Pearl opened the door for me; I remember whispering something like, "Bloody Adolph's here again then?" His car was parked outside. Pearl hushed me and I realised that Mom was coming down the stairs; she must have heard me. She looked very annoyed and she shouted at me about the state of my trousers and told me to get upstairs and change them immediately. I went up and I didn't come back out of my room until I had heard him leave. When I finally got downstairs Mom gave me a lecture about always being polite to any friends or guests who were in the house. I said that she hadn't got friends any more, just this bloke, and Mom was very angry.

She snapped that "this bloke," as I had put it, was kind and friendly to her and she said that he had tried to be exactly the same with us. I was not impressed. I just stormed away into the kitchen. There, I found that Mom had put toast and jam on the table for me and I was so annoyed about her attitude, Shipley and everything, so I just grabbed it up and threw it straight into the bin. She had followed me through and, seeing what I had done, she clipped me sharply behind the ear. She did it as if she meant it and I just turned and looked at her.

I shouted straight into her face, "You've soon forgotten about Dad, haven't you?" She hit me again and I cried and I could see that she had tears in her eyes too, so I pushed past her and shot back upstairs. I slammed the door of my bedroom behind me. It was a few minutes later, as I lay sobbing on my bed, that I heard tapping on the door but I just shouted, "Go away!" The next morning at breakfast Mom said how sorry she was and that she had never meant to hit me, but I couldn't even look her in the face.

It was at the weekend following our falling out, that Mom said that we were all going off to the Safari Park on the Sunday. Trevor immediately refused the invitation and said that he would be doing something else. I then said that I didn't want to go, but she said that there would be no one to look after us, so Pearl and I had to go. I was still feeling pretty bad about the way I had spoken to Mom and I knew that my comments that night had started the argument; perhaps I was feeling guilty and sorry for Mom at the same time. I thought that she must have discussed things with Shipley and that perhaps he was trying to endear himself towards us. Whatever the reasons, I went on Sunday and I actually enjoyed myself. Pearl and I sat in the back of the car; we both had very little to say on the way there; Shipley was not overbearing and Mom was making a special effort. Everything we asked for during the day, we were never refused it. The only time I saw Shipley get a bit grumpy was when one of the monkeys clambered onto his car and bent his car aerial over backwards. I pushed Pearl and I had to hold my hand across my mouth in order to muffle the laughter. Shipley's car seemed his pride and joy. When we got back home I remember that Mom actually got the vac out and the extension lead and took it out to Hoover the car's inside, particularly where Pearl and I had been eating crisps and cakes.

It was that same Sunday night that Trevor stayed out and then for the next two nights as well, and when he finally did come home, Mom and he had a real argument. When I say argument, well it's difficult to argue with someone who just dismisses you. It was pretty one-sided. Trevor just shrugged his shoulders in the way that only he could do it and went off up to his bedroom. I went to see where he'd been for three days; I knocked on his door gently but he didn't answer. I knocked a little louder and whispered, "It's me, Trev," and he suddenly snatched the door open.

"Well what?" he screamed.

"I just wanted to know if you were alright Trev," I asked.

"I'm fine, now sod off!"

"Where yer been?" I enquired.

"Mates, what is it with you?" he screeched.

"You're my brother Trev."

"Oh sod off wont you!" he shouted, and slammed the door shut in my face.

I went to my room and cried; I knew that he'd stopped away because of Shipley. I hated Shipley too! I wanted Trev to agree with me; I wanted us to be united and I wanted him to want me. I wanted him just to be my brother. I missed Dad's love so much and I really needed Trevor to show that we could still love one another.

After that day at the Safari Park Mom kept getting Shipley to take us out on little rides and stuff. He seemed to think that he was slowly winning us over; that he could worm his way into our lives. Sometimes he'd put his arm around me and I'd shrink away from him. He took to kissing Pearl and I used to see her wipe it away. She never admitted that her hatred was as strong as mine but I could see that she didn't like this new attention he was giving to her. There was an occasion when Mom was ironing and she had just finished pressing a pair of Pearl's knickers. Shipley picked them up and said, "These are pretty, aren't they?" I thought that he was teasing Pearl; she did not like it one bit and Mom snatched them from out of his upheld hand. He said something like, "I'm just joking ain't I?" Mom asked him not to. This was the first time that I'd ever seen Mom appear to be upset by him; but he just laughed it off. "Can't she take a bit of fun?" he enquired. Mom picked up the pile of pressed clothes, passed them to Pearl and asked her to put them away for her.

I heard Mom whisper to Pearl, "Just take no notice."

Shipley looked at me; I must have been staring at him and he shouted, "What the bloody hell you looking at?" He shot up off his stool and stomped out of the back door. He went straight off but unfortunately he came back the next day.

Shipley's visits and our outings pretty much stayed the same throughout the next twelve months. There were various occasions still when there was some tension between us, but Mom was good at forgiveness. Trevor and Pearl's birthdays came and went and mine came again; I was now eleven years of age. Shipley bought me an Albion kit. He had no interest whatsoever in football but he encouraged me. We always had low key birthdays now compared to the past. The Hullstones never came but because it was my birthday they were taking both Pearl and me bowling. Before I went Shipley asked me if I had liked his present and I said, "It's great, thanks." I didn't really know what he expected me to say but I was hardly going to say I hated it was I? He knew how much I loved the Albion. He then asked why I hadn't tried it on. I said that I didn't really need to because I knew it was the right size. He insisted that I try them on because he said that he could return it if it was wrong and get me the right sizes. I didn't want to try it but Mom gave me one of her looks and I thought, 'well, he has bought it for me and I really did want to put them on.' Mom encouraged me further by saying it would be polite to let Jack see it. I went up to my bedroom with the kit and I put it on.

When I got back down into the living room, Shipley said something like, "you're getting to be a big lad now." I felt awkward and self-conscious. Then he stood up and asked me to turn around. I asked him what for, and he replied, "So that we can see you properly." He then added, "Give us a little body-swerve."

I hesitated and said, "Don't be silly," but both Pearl and Mom said, "go on!"

What could I do? I thought I was being silly, so I just spun around. He then said, "That looks brilliant!"

Both Mom and Pearl said I looked good too, and Mom added, "You're a bit flushed Josh, are you alright, I hope you haven't got a chill coming on."

I said that I was fine. Then Mom said, "Wait until the kids at school see you in that lot, they will be green with envy!"

That night at the bowling alley I told Liam all about the new kit. Liam said that he thought that had been really kind of Jack and that perhaps he wasn't that bad after all. It must have been extremely tough for him to buy, what with him being a Wolves supporter.

"A Wolves supporter?" I replied. "He's not a Wolves supporter I don't think he supports any football at all!"

But Liam insisted that he was. He told me that his Dad had said that football had been one of the most constant arguments between my Dad and Shipley. The other apparently had been Mom.

"Mom! I don't understand, why should they have argued about Mom?"

"Well Dad said that Shipley had always insisted that your Dad had stolen your Mom from him!"

"Stolen her? I still don't understand!"

"Dad said that when they argued, Shipley insisted that he had been taking your Mom out before your Dad came along."

This was the first time that I had ever heard this and I was very annoyed and said that this made me understand why I hated him so much.

Liam agreed that he didn't really like Shipley, and he knew for a fact that his Mom and Dad didn't. But, he continued, "Perhaps he's trying to change, perhaps he is just wanting to impress you and to do the best for you; those kits are very expensive you know!"

I replied, "I know that but I didn't ask for it."

"You didn't need to ask; he knows you're an Albion fan."

"I know that, and well, I'm chuffed with the kit but the point is, don't you just think that it's strange that he's ended up with Mom after all those arguments you mentioned and I didn't know anything about this Wolves thing either?"

Liam replied, "Look, he's been with yer Mom for two years now ain't he?"

"Yeah!"

"Well don't you think that one day he's gonna become yer Dad?"

"God, I hope not!"

"I'm sorry mate but I gotta tell yer that both Mom and Dad think that he will; I've heard 'em talking about it."

I just couldn't believe that Mom would ever try to replace Dad; I was gobsmacked that Liam should even think it, or that his Mom and Dad had ever discussed it. I didn't want to even begin to imagine a new Dad, in fact there was no way that I wanted a new Dad, and after the arguing that Liam had now told me about, that went on between Dad and Shipley, well I hated him even more.

The very next day I asked Mom if she knew anything about Dad and Shipley always falling out, and she said, well of course she did.

I said, "And is it true that you and him were together?"

She hesitated slightly but then she told me that they had had just one date before she met Dad and that then there was just no contest. I couldn't stop myself from asking why she had ever got involved with him again, especially knowing that he and Dad were enemies. She replied, "They were not enemies; that's being a bit overdramatic Josh! I knew that they had differences of opinion but I don't think that they were ever enemies! I do wish you and him would try to get on better. He seems to be making an effort and he's just bought you that lovely kit, hasn't he?"

I got very angry. It's as if she was blinded to any misgiving on his part! I thought that Mom should have stayed on her own and, knowing what I now knew about Shipley, I just could not see why she would have him anywhere near her, and I also thought that it was especially disrespectful to Dad's memory. So I stormed away shouting, "I want a bolt fitted on my bedroom door!"

"A bolt, whatever for?"

"To lock the door!"

"Yes, I know perfectly well what a bolt does, but why would you want to lock your door?"

"Because I don't like the people who are in the house!"

Mom looked at me really puzzled and then, angrily, she replied, "Trevor hasn't got a lock on his door!"

"No I know, but I want one!"

She looked at me again sort of puzzled.

"Don't be so silly Josh, we always knock before we go in and out of peoples' bedrooms, don't we? I don't want you locking yourself in the room; it's dangerous."

"Yes, but…"

Mom jumped in, "Yes but nothing; you don't need one!"

I could not get her to change her mind no matter how I

tried or pleaded but I couldn't really begin to explain to her, and I was in no mood to either! It was a very difficult situation and I don't think that even Liam had understood, so how could I possibly get Mom to understand me? I started to think again about whether or not I was being too sensitive about the whole issue. I couldn't talk to her about this but it was deep within me, this very uneasy feeling. I just felt that there was something, something very strange about the whole relationship that I didn't like. It just kept on nagging at me.

The following week something else happened. I'd always been to the baths with Liam and his Dad; it was only the three of us that ever went. So I thought it extremely unusual that Shipley should suddenly suggest, right out of the blue, that he could start to take me. I immediately blurted out, "NO!" Mom was there and she asked,

"Why ever not?"

I replied, "I always go with Mr Hullstone and Liam, I always have and I always will!"

Shipley then said, "That's alright, I don't mean to stop that, I meant that I could possibly take you on another evening, just you and me."

Again I blurted out, "NO!"

"Why not?" asked Mom.

"One night a week is enough, thanks," I said. "I don't want to go any more."

Shipley tried to persuade both me and Mom that it would be a good idea, but I was adamant, no way.

Whether we liked it or not it seemed that Mom was smitten with Shipley. Any more suggestions from either Pearl or me that we didn't like him were quickly stifled. Mom always used to counteract with something like; "We'll always miss yer Dad, Jack will never replace him, I understand your feelings but Jack's a nice man." I don't really know what it was, but neither of us believed that 'Jack was a nice man.' If anything, Pearl tried her hardest, probably just to please Mom. Trevor just wanted to be left alone by everyone but there were the odd occasions of confrontation between Jack and Trevor that always led to voices being raised. Perhaps another person may not have taken so lightly such clashes of indifference. At times Shipley seemed to get very heated, but he never appeared threatening.

Trevor had now reached the age of seventeen and he was very tall and wiry; taller than Shipley by a few inches. He had several mates but none of them came to the house anymore. There were many times when Trev would come home with scratches, cuts or bruises, and Mom would ask what he'd been up to but he would never tell her. He very often sported love bites on his neck, but very rarely now did we ever see him with a girl; he'd stopped bringing them home, perhaps because he was ashamed of us, who knows? The one weekend I remember him going off to Blackpool and when he returned he had a tattoo of a lion on his right forearm; Mom was furious when she saw it. She said that Dad had never had a tattoo and that she thought they were totally disgusting.

"You'll regret it in later life!" she screamed at Trevor.

Trevor just shook his head and, once more, he sloped off to his bedroom. It was shortly after that event that Mom started to have money going missing from her purse again. I remember the one morning in the kitchen, the only time of the day when we all seemed to come together, she asked us all if we had been helping ourselves to her cash. Later on I heard her and Trevor having this one almighty argument and again he went AWOL for several days and nights. I think it was about that time when he arrived back on the scene with an old motor-scooter. Jack took one look at it and said that it wasn't roadworthy. Not to mention that Trev had no road tax for it. I didn't really understand much of this event but I do know that it all led again to several scenes between the three of them. Trevor resented Shipley ever taking any part in such family discussions. He would very often shout, "You're not my BLOODY DAD!" He would repeat this over and over again always warning Shipley to "butt out!" Such events always ended up with Mom in a flood of tears.

About three months before my twelfth birthday, Mom, Shipley, Pearl and I were all sat around the dinner table. It was not very often that we were this formal but Mom did occasionally like to do this. I really didn't want to sit with Shipley at any time but I loved Mom and I tried to keep the peace. Mom and Shipley were all smiles; laughing and joking and there were moments when we were all giggling for some forgotten and probably very silly reason. Then, right out of the blue, Mom suddenly announced, "Jack has asked me to marry him!"

I must admit that there was such a deathly silence. It was just has Liam had kept saying and the moment I never wanted to happen. Mom repeated as if we hadn't heard her properly: "Jack has asked me to marry him…Well, what do you have to say?"

I, for one, had such a lot, but nothing that I wanted to say in front of Jack. I must have given a tortured smile but I think Pearl actually kissed Jack upon the cheek and then she threw her arms around Mom's neck. I must have been sitting there in shock; it was as though someone had just smacked me in the face with a cricket bat. Oh God, NO, I thought. But oh God, Yes! It was going to happen! I got up and took my ball out into the garden and belted the living daylights out of it. It was a wonder the shed didn't collapse with the ferocity of the force and battering that it took. I don't know how long it was before Jack came out but immediately I saw him I just screeched, "I need the toilet," and I ran back inside.

Worse was still to happen when Trevor was told of their decision. He was absolutely furious and he said a lot of cruel and nasty things to Mom. I believe that she had purposely chosen to tell him when Jack was not around and of course this gave Trevor the chance to unleash his venom. Both Pearl and I ended up in tears along with Mom. Trevor told Mom that she had never loved Dad and even accused her of having seen Jack before Dad's death, (Which I knew now to be true). He said that he hated Jack but that most of all he hated her. When he had finished shouting and screaming at her in his loudest voice, he calmly stated that he would be out of this dump, (referring to our house), as quickly as he possibly could. Following this incident the atmosphere in the house was never the same again. Whenever Trevor was home you could cut the tension with a knife and never knew when the situation would flare up again. Shipley and Trevor were like the same poles of a magnet totally repelled from one another. If Shipley did have the audacity to even attempt to speak to Trevor it would end in a violent verbal clash. Trevor left Jack without illusion; there would never ever be a truce whilst he had breath in his body.

I was present when Mom told Mr and Mrs Hullstone and, as there had been before with Pearl and I, there was a short period of awkward silence. The first words spoken were not congratulatory words but inquisitive and concerned.

Mrs Hullstone asked, "Are you certain this is what you want Floss?"

Mom assured them both that it was exactly what she wanted; there was another awkward silence, then no celebration followed, they just wished her good luck. Liam and I left them to it and went into the garden and his first words to me were, "I'm sorry mate." I knew exactly what he meant but there was none sorrier than me. Liam then enquired, "Are you seeing eye to eye with him now?"

"No better, no worse!" I replied. I was lying and I knew it as soon as the words left my mouth, when I added, "If Mom thinks he's okay then perhaps he is." The words stuck in my throat.

I think that Liam understood me as well as I understood myself. He knew that I had these concerns about Shipley but he also knew that I had no real justification for them.

Following the formal announcement, it took Shipley the minimal amount of time to establish himself in our home. Mom had a new ring on her finger but, worse still, she had taken Dad's off. I remember, after noticing this, when there was no one else around, I went into Mom's bedroom and found Dad's rings in her little trinket box. I clutched them tightly in my hand and cried. There was a full-length picture of Mom and Dad on their wedding day hung on the wall, and I looked into Dad's eyes and I said, "I'm sorry." I don't know why I needed to say this, but I did. I put the rings back where I had found them after a few minutes of tears and then I left the room quietly, touching Dad's hand as I left.

From that time onwards Trevor used the house as a Hotel/B&B. He came and went; saying very little, sometimes just sleeping at home and leaving in the morning. Then for some reason, the one Friday night, he arrived at the house at about eight o'clock, grabbed something to eat from the kitchen and went straight to his bedroom. The next few days he was about and we used to just bump into one another occasionally on the landing or stairs. He had given up on any conversation or even a grunt at this stage; not even a nod of the head. I seemed to be invisible to him and I knew, perhaps as a brother does know, that all was not well with Trevor. I mean, not our normal trouble, something else was seriously troubling Trevor. Unfortunately I was proven to be only too right when the Police came calling on us again. I wasn't there at the time; I was at school when they arrived but eventually I heard the whole story. It seems they arrived and Mom wasn't even aware if Trevor was in the house. He was in his bedroom and Mom, unaware, and mainly for the Police to see her willingness to cooperate, kept shouting out his name. He didn't answer or show himself. The officers then produced a warrant, entered the house, went to his bedroom and tried to open the door. This was barricaded so they burst it open and had to wrestle him to the floor. By now Mom was hysterical, and Mrs Gould, having seen the police, and heard the rumpus, came to check that all was well and to comfort Mom. Neither of them at that moment had any idea whatsoever what Trevor had supposed to have done but the officers were definitely in no mood to be messed about with.

Trevor was dragged away from the house, handcuffed and bundled into the police car. The news about the arrest appeared on the front page of the Express and Star, and Mom was left shocked and ashamed. It emerged that Trevor had supposedly been involved in some sort of 'smash and grab' raid on the Sparks electrical store. Along with two other so-called accomplices he had stolen a car, smashed into the glazed doorway of the store and robbed it. The car was said later to have been dumped on wasteland by the canal and set on fire. Mom was allowed to visit Trevor at the local cop-shop, and she told us that he was in a terrible state, really very upset and sorry for what he had done and that he had not meant to bring Mom all of this worry. It was difficult to imagine Trevor having been crying openly to Mom but apparently he had. He was back at home by mid-week escorted by a plain-clothed police lady; she had been made responsible for him and Mom had to give assurances that he would not abscond whilst awaiting the court hearing.

When I first saw him he looked so frail and afraid; I wanted to hug him and ask him, 'why?' But Trevor was still Trevor; there was still something very dark and sinister about him. It was a very disturbing thought, but he was still my brother and I loved him. I wanted so much to understand him; why would, why does anyone, do anything like this. Why did Trevor feel the need to do it; surely he had no valid reason? Shipley condemned him. He wanted him out. He told Mom that he was a 'bad un' and that she'd never do any good with him. Trevor was there and he said nothing to vindicate himself. For days, Mom took Trevor food on a tray up into his bedroom. She collected his dirty clothes and delivered him clean ones. Several times I heard her trying to discuss things with him and I heard Trevor repeat over and over again, "Sorry, sorry, sorry!" Mom cried a lot but Trevor was still hard. Trevor was not sorry for himself; he was sorry for us. It seemed to take forever for the trial day to arrive and the atmosphere around the house was toxic. When it finally did come, it resulted in Trevor getting a six month custodial sentence. I cried, Pearl cried and Mom cried. Shipley was there to support Mom but never once did he display any connection or emotion. There was one good thing that came out of all of this misery (not that Shipley saw it this way) but the wedding date had to be delayed. Mom was adamant that it would not happen without Trevor; the contradiction in this being that I knew, and I think Mom knew too, that Trevor still would not be there for them on their day!

Unfortunately during the period of time Trevor was

away, and due to the delayed wedding, Shipley spent much more time at our home and I began to know the man better than ever. It seemed as if he had a complex; sometimes he was deep and dark, not speaking for long periods of time. He moaned about the smallest of irritations and seemed to take fun out of plaguing Pearl and me. He was very possessive of Mom and seemed to be extremely jealous when she paid too much interest in either of us. He was forever commenting about the way, he thought, she doted upon us. He would say that she spoiled us and that we should do more for ourselves and more about the house. He would get into silly little niggles with Mom. All in all, he was a very irritating man. He also began to argue more and more with Mom as time progressed and he hated the fact that he had had to delay the wedding for her precious criminal son!

Shipley's attitude caused me to question even more greatly Mom's reasoning for wanting to be with this horrible person, but whenever I ventured anywhere near the subject she would become annoyed with me. On one occasion she cried and told me that she had no intentions of living the rest of her life on her own and becoming a "miserable old widow woman!" I said that she had us; Trevor, Pearl and I, but she replied that we wouldn't be about forever and that we would go our own ways. She begged for my understanding and from then on I tried to withhold my opinion about the man I distrusted and had no love for. He ridiculed Pearl and me at times and he embarrassed us whenever he got the opportunity. He threatened us with backhanders should we have the audacity to answer him back and it was not long before I realised, that he was a drunk!

I remember the one day that I arrived home from school to find Mom sporting a badly bruised eye. She said that she had walked into the open door. I did not believe her for one minute and I knew that if Trevor had been at home then Shipley would have been in trouble. I told her that I thought that it was Shipley and she just started to cry. She said, "Oh not again Josh please; I walked into the door, please don't make matters worse." I put my arms around her and held her tightly; I loved her very much and I too had tears in my eyes. If I were older and stronger I would have killed Shipley for this. When Pearl arrived, I stopped her in the hallway and told her; she tried to push past me but I told her not to start Mom again, to tread carefully because Mom seemed really worked up about the matter.

I heard her asking Mom about her eye and Mom repeated the same words that she had said to me earlier. Fortunately Pearl accepted her words, didn't make a fuss about it and said that she should take more care. I avoided saying another word because I had already upset Mom and I didn't want to start again. I was dreading Shipley's return though because I didn't think that I'd be able to look him in the face without telling him what I thought of him! As it happened, we didn't see him that night because he didn't come home. Mom said nothing at the breakfast table but I knew that when Shipley returned in one of his drunken states he always made too much noise about the place; banging and clattering, he wanted people to know that he was there.

Unfortunately for all of us, when I returned from school that day Shipley was sat there once more, legs straddled across the fireplace, taking up more than his fair share of space. When I went into the kitchen there was a large bunch of flowers decorating the window sill (obviously a peace offering). I sensed that the atmosphere was still icy! Shipley made small talk but I tried avoiding him and when Pearl arrived she seemed to be giving him a wide berth too. It was a few days before things began to settle down and, slowly, the wedding talk started to drift back into the conversation. Wedding talk! They must have lost their senses! There were nights when I lay in bed listening to the raised voices and there were times when I heard Mom's tears. She had certainly bitten off more than she could chew and didn't know how to spit it out!

Then the day came that we were all sent home for the half-day because of the heating going down at school. I knew that Mom wouldn't be home because she always visited her sister (Aunt Mary) on the Friday afternoons when we were at school. It was a ritual that she had carried on for many years. Shipley, I thought, should have been at work. His car wasn't around when I arrived and all seemed quiet as I opened the front door. I was taking my school coat off in the hall and I had just hung my bag upon one of the coat hooks at the bottom of the stairway. It was then that I heard a voice from upstairs. It was a woman's voice, and I nearly, instinctively shouted out, 'is that you Mom?' But then I heard Shipley; I hadn't recognised the woman's words but he was saying, "Hurry up back!" I held back from the bottom of the stairs because, suddenly, I saw the owner of the first voice cross the landing heading into the toilet. The woman I saw was naked and had long blonde hair. She didn't look around and was totally unaware of my presence. I stood there, frozen, until the door began to open back up, and I leant back in tightly towards the hall wall. I could hear them in my Mother's bedroom; messing about, giggling and whatever else! I must have been there for about fifteen minutes until I decided that I had better get out of there. The last thing that I wanted was for Shipley to become aware of me being there. I slowly slid my coat back on and lifted my bag cautiously from its hook, twisted the door-knob and clicked the door silently behind me. I kept away until my normal home time and then returned. It was thirty minutes or more before Shipley's arrival.

Mom was sat at the kitchen table reading a book. I asked her if she'd been to Aunt Mary's and she replied, "Yes!" She then said, "Oh she's sent you and Pearl a Mars each, they're on there," pointing in the direction of the kitchen shelf. I picked up one of the Mars bars and sat down alongside her. I began to unwrap it but she said, "No, don't eat it now it'll spoil your tea!"

Suddenly, I couldn't hold back and I just blurted out, "He's had a woman in here!"

Mom sat there just staring at me as if I'd gone mad. So I repeated it.

"I said; he's had a woman in here!"

"I know what you said but you're not making any sense!"

"Jack's had a woman in here!" I spoke slowly and deliberately; how could she not understand me?

"We were sent home from school just after our lunch-break because the heating had broken, and Jack was here with a woman."

It was silent for just a few moments before Mom spoke again.

"Jack's at work, he's not even been home yet."

"Are you saying that you don't believe me Mom?"

"I don't understand why you keep wanting to make this trouble for him!"

I was getting angry now.

"What's the matter with you Mom, what's it gonna take for you to see sense? Jack's a drunk, a liar, a thug and a womaniser!"

Mom stood up angrily and raising her voice, she said, "Shut up! ...Shut up!"

I pleaded with her, "Oh Mom, please don't, what's it

need to open your eyes up? Jack had a blonde woman up in your bedroom when I got home. His car was nowhere to be seen. I was here for at least fifteen minutes without them even knowing and they were in the room all that time. I saw her walk across the landing naked!"

Mom slapped me across my face and burst into tears!

I ran for my room without another word being spoken.

CHAPTER SIX
The Wedding

Trevor came home eventually; it was not the full six months but it seemed like forever. In the meantime I'd been experiencing a lot more bullying at school; some kids think it's fun to laugh at others' misfortunes. To them I was now the convict's brother. They'd taunt me by forever asking how the jailbird was doing. They would ask me when I was going to join him. They'd shout after me down the street and I had to learn to harden to it. I toughened up; I hated and I hit back. Mom was called into school. I got punished so I hardened some more. At home I became spiteful with Pearl and I shouted and screamed at Mom. There were times when Shipley dragged me to my bedroom and shut me in; forbidding me to return until I came back to my senses. Trevor returned home seeming softer, repentant but no more amiable. I think that he had probably spent some of his time locked up praying for Shipley's departure before his return but saw that this was simply pie in the sky. I still hoped for Shipley's departure and sometimes I even wished for more than that, sometimes I'd stand in the kitchen with the sharpest knife I could find in the drawer, clasped firmly in my hand, and nurtured very dark thoughts. It was only a month after Trevor's return that Mom announced the new wedding date of August the third.

After a long period of hibernation Trevor eventually started to venture out again. His accomplices were all now out of prison and Mom worried every second he was away. Shipley occasionally confronted and threatened him; Trevor said very little. I left little gifts for him in his bedroom but he never said a word; sometimes he would give me a meaningful look, a wink or a nod. It was a glimmer of light; a slight crack in the armour. Somewhere inside that hard shell there was my brother trying to escape and I would never give up on the eventuality of that success. Mom's love for Shipley was all that parted all four of us. It parted Mom from her three children and that toxic hatred that it created drove wedges between us three. Always somewhere in the depths of my mind I had this memory; this yearning, this burning desire to be back as we all once were. Why had this had to happen to our family? Why had Dad died in the way that he had? Why had Mom chosen this vile person, of all people, to replace him? Shipley would never replace Dad. I would never call him Dad and I knew that Trevor would never break his silence or be rid of the hatred that he felt towards him. Pearl, well, she still tried. I know it was for Mom's sake alone, just to keep the peace, but she too disliked Shipley.

As the wedding drew nearer and the weeks were counted down it seemed that only Mom had any pleasure from the plans that were being made. I really did not want to be there and Trevor had already stated that he would be somewhere else on that day. Where? Well, anywhere that wasn't at the wedding. For their honeymoon Mom and Shipley were going off for a week's holiday in Blackpool; this meant that Pearl and I were being shipped out elsewhere, namely the Hullstones' house, which I thought was fantastic and couldn't wait to get there. It was during the main school holiday so it meant that we would have nothing else to do and a week spent with Liam was just the answer. The Hullstones were coming to the wedding; I suppose they had no option really, but privately Liam had told me that they were not over enthusiastic about the whole thing. Of course Trevor wasn't going to the Hullstones; he was old enough to look after himself, so he had made clear to Mom. He had made plans to stay at Corey's house; that was one of his old mates from school. He used to visit our house at times and they would blast out rock music together. Mom didn't particularly like Corey but he was the better of some evils in her opinion. Shipley had had run-ins with Trevor and Corey before but he was sick of Trevor by now.

Mom took Pearl and me shopping. She said that we would have to get everything new to be just perfect. Pearl was to be a 'maid of honour', or some other such nonsense, and Mom had wanted me to be a paige boy but I had totally refused to do it. She still wanted me dressed for the part; so she bought me a navy-blue pin-striped suit with a little waistcoat. I remembered that day especially because I had to sit and watch Pearl go in and out of one changing room after another. She came out dressed in all sorts of weird and wonderful outfits until finally she and Mom were in full agreement and I was bored rigid. I chose the first pair of shoes that I saw and liked; it took Pearl about forty five minutes to get hers. Mom also meant what she had said about everything new because that day we also had new underwear. Mom had more or less begged Trev to come and he was adamant that he would not. Mom did give Trevor enough money though to go out and kit himself up. He kept repeating, "I won't be there" and Mom just kept saying, "oh, well take it anyway!" Eventually he accepted the money but I can't remember seeing him in anything new.

As the day was almost upon us the tension grew around the house. Trevor went out of his way to upset Shipley; he lived in hope that he could still drive him away. He had one or two slanging matches with Mom as well until the one day when I found myself brave enough to tell him to back off and cool it; but he pushed me onto my backside using the force of both hands. I had tears in my eyes, not for me but for Trevor; he was fighting a lost cause and really he knew I supported him in that cause, but he was hurting Mom too. I didn't want Mom to keep being on the sharp edge of things. Pearl tried to act as a peacemaker between us; she cried a lot and begged us to be happy for Mom and to give her our support. She said that all the arguments in the world would never bring Dad back, and she was right.

With it now being closed season for the football, I was seeing a little bit less of the Hullstones. I still went swimming with Liam and his Dad but unless I was allowed to go around to Liam's house, they no longer visited us as they had at one time. I sometimes believed that Liam, as good a friend as he was, must have been fed up with the ever constant whinging about Shipley. At times I bombarded him with the arguments and the nasty atmosphere that surrounded my life. To be fair to Liam he always listened well and seemed to share my sorrow in the way things had turned out at home. Sometimes he would ask if I remembered the surfers on Chapel Porth beach, and of course I would say "Yes" and then he would say, "Remember when the waves threw them twenty feet or so into the air and their boards would come crashing down upon them?" and I said, "Yes it was brilliant to see." Then he would remind me that, at the time, I had called them maniacs but, no matter how many times they had come tumbling down, they would always come back up again; struggling against the tide, clambering back onto their boards and again ride high. His point was that I should do the same!

Two days before the wedding day arrived, Trevor went missing. Mom asked everywhere she could think that he may be and because of her anxiety, Shipley went off in search of him but found no trace. His friends knew nothing, or they were saying nothing. Mom discovered that he had packed a bag and taken lots of his stuff.

"Where the hell has he gone?" she asked me as if she thought I was aware.

To which I jumped back, "Don't take it out of me!"

"I'm not taking it out of you Josh; I'm sorry, I know it's not your fault."

In retaliation I added, "If I was any older I wouldn't be here either!"

Desperately Mom asked, "Why can't you all just let things go; I loved your Dad, Jack will never replace your Dad, he knows and understands that!"

"Well he'll never be my Dad anyway!" I blurted out.

"He knows that too; give him a chance, why don't you. What has he ever done to harm any of you?"

So the wedding day came; Trevor did not come home and did not show for the wedding. As far as the day could go I suppose everything was more or less perfect for Mom; she looked beautiful in her dress and so did Pearl in hers (well, as much as sisters can look good). I spent all of my time with the Hullstones, Liam especially, and we enjoyed ourselves. The wedding took place at the registrar office; the photographs after took far too long but the reception, well that was great. Jack knew this band that used to play the local pub circuit; they were called 'The Pumpkin Seeds'. They consisted of three guitarists, a keyboard player and a drummer. When they took their half-time break I asked the drummer if I could have a go on the drums and he showed me a few moves then left me to it. I had always wanted to sit behind a full set of drums like that and I loved it. Liam got to have a go to; we both thought it was musical heaven but it was probably a din. I believe I was the better of the two of us and Liam agreed. Some of the grown-ups asked us to come off initially but unfortunately for them the drummer said that it was fine. Pearl got to dance with one or two of the lads there and seemed to be gathering admirers due to her clothes; they did make her look older. I'd never seen Pearl in this way before; she looked to be maturing. Even Liam asked her for a dance but she refused him and he was a bit put out by it.

Mom and Shipley left the reception at about ten o'clock. Some of their friends, and I suspect the neighbours, had tied strings and cans to the back bumper of Jack's car. I expected that being his pride and joy, it would upset Jack but they left them on and went off down the road with the cans rattling and scraping. Right after their departure, Mrs Hullstone suggested that we might leave but us kids mainly wanted to stay on and Mr Hullstone said, "Come on we don't very often get a night out, we're on holiday too and now that they've gone let's enjoy it!"

Mrs Hullstone said, "Watch what you're saying in front of the kids." But he didn't need to keep it from us.

It was probably about 12.15am when we left the centre. The band had just finished off with the last waltz and Liam and I had sat taking the mickey out of his parents and the rest of the smoochers on the dance floor. Pearl had worn herself out; she was slumped in a corner complaining that she'd eaten and drunk too much. I hadn't been up this late for ages but I didn't seem tired at all. All I could think about was the following week; spending all this time with my mate, sharing his bedroom, and having a great time without thinking once about Shipley.

On the Sunday morning Liam and I didn't get up until well after 11.00am. Pearl and Mrs Hullstone were sitting out in the garden by their fish pond. The sun was shining and it was a beautiful day.

"Come on sleepy heads!" was the greeting we received

from Mrs Hullstone, and Pearl added, “What time d’yer call this?”

Liam asked, “Why what time is it?”

“Twenty minutes past eleven!” Replied his Mom.

Liam replied, “That ain’t late fer a Sunday Mom.”

“It’s late enough; what d’yer want for your breakfast, shall I do beans on toast?”

“Yes please Mom,” Liam replied and then added, “Is that alright Josh?”

I said, “Yes, thank you Mrs Hullstone, anything that ain’t any trouble; what’s Pearl had?”

“She’s had the same.”

Pearl butted in, “But I was up at about tenish!”

Then Mrs Hullstone added, “Yeah, just after us, we were late ourselves.”

She gave me a smile enough to say, ‘don’t worry I’m only pulling your leg.’ and I asked, “Did you enjoy yourselves?”

“Yes thank you Josh; it was a good night wasn’t it?”

She was standing and on her way into the kitchen and I asked, “Has Mom phoned yet?”

She gave a little chuckle and replied, “No, give her chance, she won’t be in touch yet, she’s probably up late too.”

From up the garden we heard a voice shout, “Come on lazybones, we could have been over ‘the rec’.” It was Mr Hullstone.

Mrs Hullstone must have heard him from the kitchen and she poked her head out of the doorway and shouted,

“Take no notice of him lads; he ain’t in any fit state to be over the Rec.”

Just after, she called us to say that the beans were ready but Liam asked if we could sit outside and eat them, she replied,

"Of course you can." And she brought a tray out to us.

We all sat around the pool and Mr Hullstone came and joined us. We ate our beans watching the koi carp dodge about in and out of the shade. I threw little crumbs of toast into the water and they jostled and jumped about for it.

Mr Hullstone said, "Don't give 'em too much Josh, they're fat enough as it is."

At around one o'clock Pearl went to help Mrs Hullstone to prepare the Sunday lunch. Mrs Hullstone had earlier put a joint of lamb into the oven and now they were starting to prepare the vegetables; she shouted out to Mr Hullstone, "About 3 o'clock should be fine, shouldn't it?"

"Yeah of course it is, I'll come in and get us all a drink. You get back out here and enjoy this sun, there's no rush, we're on holiday."

Liam asked his Dad what he'd got planned for us during the week and he answered, "Anything and everything!"

I said, "It's great that you're off, Mr Hullstone, because we'd have been lost without you."

He replied, "Yeah, I asked the boss and we weren't too busy so it wasn't a problem to get the week, I'm looking forward to it too."

"What d'yer mean anything and everything, Dad?"

"Well fishing, swimming, football, bowling, pictures, anything and everything!"

"Josh ain't bothered about fishing, you know that Dad."

"Well that's only one thing ain't it?"

I jumped in with, "No! It's alright Mr Hullstone, I'd love to go fishing for a change, it's been ages anyway and it's not all about me, is it?"

"Would you?" asked Liam, sounding very shocked and surprised at my statement, and I replied,

"Yeah, course I would, I'm gonna enjoy every minute

of this week."

Then Liam enquired, "Oh! How about Pearl, Dad?"

"Well, she can do whatever she wants to do with us lads and then I'm sure her and Ma will spend time doing things, like shopping." He shouted in, "Ain't that right Ma?"

"What's right?"

"You and Pearl doing some shopping?"

Mrs Hullstone smiled at Pearl and Pearl smiled back and nodded yes. Mrs Hullstone replied, "Yes, I'm sure we will."

Needless to say we had a great week; I felt my age again. I didn't have all the baggage of those grown-up worries. Mr Hullstone was like my Dad; he enjoyed life without the complications. The Hullstones had a large picture of Mom and Dad over their sideboard and Liam's Dad saw me standing next to it the one day, staring at it, and he said, "He was a fine man."

I turned to look at him and he repeated, "He was a fine man yer Dad, they made a lovely couple. You're getting to look a lot like him Josh."

"You were friends for a good many years weren't you, Mr Hullstone?"

"Yes Josh, I respected and admired yer Dad; he was an honest, hard-working man, he didn't deserve to have what happened to him."

The two things did not go together but suddenly I said, "I don't like Jack, Mr Hullstone!"

"I know son, it's pretty obvious that none of you do. Neither do I but let's not mention him in the same breath as your Dad son, it's not befitting."

"I miss him every day." I could feel the emotion swelling inside of me and it was so good to be able to be honest and talk openly with someone who shared my thoughts.

Mr Hullstone replied, “I know son and we do too; we’ll always miss him.”

“We won’t be a proper family again, never!” I said with hate in my heart.

“Yer Mom’s gotta move on, son, it’s a lonely life.”

“She’s got us three kids, Mr Hullstone; that should be enough.”

“No! It’s not son, you’ll understand as you get a little older yourself; don’t feel too bad towards yer Mom, she deserves some happiness son.”

“But we’re all unhappy Mr Hullstone.”

Mr Hullstone placed his arm around my shoulders. His touch was not like that of Shipley’s; I found his warmth and his empathy; he had real love for us.

“Time is a great healer son and things might not work out as bad as we all think. You’ve got us; we’ll always be here for you and Pearl and Trevor. You’ll always be welcome in my house son, any child of Franks would be.”

Surprisingly I found myself confirming, “Trevor as well, Mr Hullstone?”

“Yes, even Trev, he can’t be held responsible for what’s happening in his life at the moment; he’s got himself a little lost Josh, but he’ll find himself again, I know that he will and we should give him all the support that we can.”

During that week we crammed in all that we could; Mr Hullstone was tireless and wouldn’t rest until we had gone through his list and some more. Liam and I had some separate time to ourselves and we had all the time as a family; I enjoyed all of it. We did go fishing on the one day and strangely enough, and quite amusingly (for me that was), I caught more fish than anyone. It helped that the sun shone all week so there was nothing to stop us. Whenever Mrs Hullstone and Pearl wanted time out they just went off and did their own thing. All of us went to see the new film, ‘Lassie’, and that was probably the only time that tears were shed all week although Mr Hullstone kept denying that he had cried, but I saw him wipe away a tear. As the week drew closer to its end the fear of the return to *my* life started to dawn upon me, especially having to spend time with Jack permanently around the house. Mom rang us twice during that week; I spoke to her on both occasions and she said that they were having a good time and she hoped that we were too. She was still very concerned about Trevor because we had heard nothing from him and neither had she. I was relaxed about the situation really; I somehow knew that Trev was okay. He being away hadn’t affected my week at all; I’d had little time to be concerned for him and I thought that he would be back as always; Trevor could look after himself, I knew that!

CHAPTER SEVEN

Shipley Moves In

"If he ain't back by the end of this week, then he can bloody well stay away!" declared Shipley.

"No, don't say that Jack, he'll always be welcome here it's his home."

"Yer too bloody soft with 'em; that's why he treats you like a ruddy door mat!"

"He doesn't treat me like anything, they've had a lot to put up with and it's hurt us all."

"Don't keep dwelling on that every bloody five minutes; you ain't the only ones who've had problems in yer life!"

"I know that Jack, but please try for me, won't you, just give 'em some time and space."

I sat at the top of the stairs just listening to them going on; he hadn't been in the house five minutes and he was already trying to lay the law down. As it happened Trevor arrived back home that very same night; he went straight upstairs, put his things in his bedroom and behaved as if he'd never been away.

The following morning I remember going into Mom's room; I think I was looking for a biro, she usually had one or two lying around on her bedside cabinet. I was right; I think that I'd got a choice of three. Anyway, I snatched one up and went to turn away when something caught my eye at the side of the bed. I knew Mom lay on the side where the cabinet was but this was on what I now presumed was Shipley's side. So, I went around to take a closer look and realised that it was an old baseball bat. It was stood between the bed and the old chimney breast wall; in the recess. But what was it doing there? I'd never seen it before. I took a look at it; it was an old worn out thing. It had some old cord or something twisted around the handle end; then I noticed that just below the grip there were two sharp notches cut into the neck of the bat. The notches formed a sort of 'v' shape and were almost identical; they had been cut with a sharp blade, they definitely weren't just scrapes. One of them seemed older than the other; I could tell this because of the colouring of the wood. It was a strange thing to place beside your bed; perhaps Shipley used to play baseball? I replaced it back carefully where I had found it and returned to my room. Later that same morning I asked Mom about it and she said that it was Shipley's bat.

"Had he used to play baseball then, Mom?" I asked.

"No silly, at least I don't think so. He just keeps it for safety."

"Safety; what d'yer mean safety?"

"Well he says that if we ever had a break in he'd use it."

"But we ain't ever had a break in!"

"No, I know that."

"Is he frightened then Mom?"

"No, don't be silly, it's just in case."

"Did Dad ever keep anything then Mom?"

"No of course he didn't!"

"How d'yer mean, 'course he didn't', people could have broken in then, couldn't they?"

"Yes I suppose they could have, but they didn't Josh, and Dad never bothered about such things."

"Why's he got two notches carved into it?"

"You ask the funniest questions; why's who got two notches carved in what?"

"Two notches in the baseball bat handle, haven't yer looked at it?"

"No! Of course I ain't it's just a bat!"

"He's got two notches carved into the handle of it."

"Well, I don't know why; what have you been looking at it for anyway, just go and play, I'm trying to sort the dinner out."

The notches were a mystery but I soon forgot about them and the bat. I went out into the garden and kicked the ball about a bit again.

It was not the same house that I had been used to living in. Mom paid Jack an awful lot of attention and mainly left us to get on with our own lives. Trevor continued to come and go at his own convenience and Pearl began to spend more and more time next-door with Mrs Gould, but I could see that she was not happy. Pearl and Mom had been so close in the past, it must have seemed like a huge wrench being parted so often from her. I suppose that we were just growing up and that nothing stays the same. I was even glad to be starting back to school soon, even if we were going into old battleaxe's class. At least Liam and I would see each other every day and, whenever I could get to go back to have tea at his house, then I would take it. Mr Hullstone would always drop me off later at home (the later the better).

When a routine had become established at home, and Shipley and Mom had started to forget the honeymoon, things began to become even more tense around the house. Shipley regularly arrived home from work in a foul mood. He didn't appear to like his job at all even though I had overheard Mom telling Mrs Gould that he was in a better paid job than Dad had been. He definitely drank more booze than Dad ever did, and he would regularly turn up late after work the worse for it. Dad used to drink occasionally but

Shipley regularly went straight to the pub after finishing his job and it was obvious that Shipley overdid it. Even when he arrived home earlier he would sometimes bribe one or the other of us kids to go and fetch him some drink from the off-license. Shipley kept two of the large brown cider bottles and he would get us to take these to have filled with Banks's bitter. He always finished these off before he turned in for bed. He had to bribe us as none of us wanted to do anything for him, he was such a misery. Although he and Trevor never exchanged polite words, if he put the 'bribe money' and the bottles ready on the table even Trevor fetched it. It cost Shipley dear but drink very often shut up his whingeing. Trevor and Shipley's relationship had not improved one iota; they argued incessantly and Mom had become a skilful referee, very often having to get between them to calm down the confrontations. Another change was that Shipley used bad language around the house and I can never in my memory remember having heard Dad swear.

Shipley kept a bottle of Bells' Whisky on the top shelf of the kitchen cupboard and I became aware that our Trevor was starting to help himself to it. I caught him out on one or two occasions standing on a chair taking swigs from the bottle. Of course Shipley was never about on these occasions and I don't believe he ever questioned where the drink was going. I remember though that Trev always behaved a little sillier after he had been at the bottle. Sometimes he would do handstands up against the kitchen sink until all of his face would go blood red. He was also stealing Shipley's cigarettes whenever he managed to get his hands on them. It wasn't very often that I saw him do this but on a few of the occasions he would offer me a quick puff of one and I used to feel sick; he said my face turned pea green. Pearl found out and threatened to tell Mom about us if she ever caught us again. Trev wasn't only naughty at home he was also getting into more and more scrapes out and about and at school too. I knew that there were days when he would just hang around along the canal or he would go to the park with a few mates rather than going looking for any work. I started to leave my homework at times, and Mom no longer checked up on us the way that she had on earlier occasions. The teachers at school became more and more annoyed with me and shouted at me incessantly.

The time passed by so quickly; I don't believe that there were many days when I didn't give a passing thought to my Dad, Cornwall and St Agnes. Mom didn't fuss around us so much and there were times when Pearl's P.E. kit was not ready for her; that would never have happened in the past. When Shipley and Mom went out together we always got dumped on the neighbours, and Trevor was left a free-agent; he just roamed around the area and did what he did. Quite frequently we had knocks upon the door and it would be someone complaining to either Mom or the neighbours about Trev's behaviour. It was after one of these occasions that a neighbour had caught the flak from Trev's indulgencies, that Shipley finally cracked big time. He waited for Trev to get back home and then he caught hold of him by the scruff of his neck and flung him about; there was a lot of shouting and swearing and eventually Shipley landed Trevor a backhander. Trevor fell against the table and banged his head. When he rose to his feet he threatened that he would kill Shipley if he ever laid a finger on him again.

"Don't ever, ever hit me again!" he blasted.

"Shut your bloody mouth or I'll give you another!"

Trevor swaggered in front of him, bobbing about like a prize fighter whilst all the time Mom was screaming and shouting for them to stop. I really wanted to see Trevor land one on him and Mom had to keep a firm grip upon me.

"Come on then!" Trev taunted. "You won't be so bloody lucky the next time!"

Mom finally pushed me to one side and forced her way between them, pushing Jack backwards. Trevor, feeling very brave, tried to get around her, and Mom tussled with him too. Then Trev accidentally stepped on Mom's foot causing her to cry out; he hadn't meant to hurt her so he flew passed her and up the stairs to his room. The following day there were still angry words spoken and distances kept and I heard Trevor pleading with Mom to get rid of Jack before it was too late; I didn't really understand, when what was too late?

This encounter did lead me to trust Jack even less although I had always had a lack of faith. I began to become even more aware of him; I didn't like the way his eyes seemed to follow me about the place and his hands always wanted to be patting me or touching me, I used to flinch away from him. With Pearl he seemed to want to be tickling her whenever she got anywhere near him, and I noticed that he was always making comments about her becoming grown-up and the way she needed new clothes to fit her curves. Pearl was regularly embarrassed by Jack's comments and now it was obvious that, even at the risk of upsetting Mom, Pearl was becoming sick of his constant unwanted attention. Her patience was obviously running dry. She snapped regularly and asked him to leave her alone; she even pleaded with Mom to get him to stop tormenting her and she said that he was weird but Mom still insisted that it was only a little bit of harmless fun.

We actually went away on holiday together the following summer to Weymouth. It took a lot of persuasion from Mom to get Pearl and me to go; neither of us wanted to spend a week cooped up with Jack. Trevor wouldn't come, no matter what the persuasion, and Mom gave up in the end. Her terms were, that Trev could stay at home but that Mrs Talbot must have a key to the house, and she had agreed to ensure that Trev got one cooked meal every day because she was concerned about his lack of eating. Trev had lost some weight and he generally looked pale. If my hopes had been that this holiday would be anything like that in Cornwall then I was to be sorely disappointed. Fortunately I had no real aspirations because, truth is, I did not want to be there. Shipley and Mom ended up doing a lot of things themselves and leaving Pearl and me to our own devices. We did all go down to the beach together every day, but this beach was pebbly, not like the golden sands I'd seen in Cornwall. The weather was excellent so that was a bonus and Pearl and I got to go into the sea and the pool every day. We also got to chat a lot more about Shipley and some of his weird ways; Pearl agreed with me that he made us both feel very uncomfortable at times. He was not family to us, and both of us changed our clothes behind the locked shower room door. When we were in his presence with our costumes on he seemed to stare at us; Pearl agreed with me on that. I always kept a distance between me and him. It was only the second time that I had my trunks on in his company when he made some comment about my pubic hair showing above my trunks; you know, just up to my belly button. I had not been too conscious or concerned about it but he seemed to be making fun of me and it made me more conscious of my appearance. I didn't understand what was unusual, or indeed if there was anything unusual at all. Afterwards I said something to Mom about his comments, and she just said, "Oh, don't be silly, it's just Jack, he's just being playful." But each day after that first remark he didn't let it go, he had to make some stupid remark.

When we got back home from our holiday Trevor had made a bit of a mess of the house and Shipley went berserk again. Firstly he found what could have been red wine stains on the carpet, in the living room, and when he took some stuff out to the bin, he found broken glasses in there. His head blew though when he switched on the living room light and there were dark shadows cast about the room, that turned out to be cocktail sausages in the glass chandelier. Mom spoke to Mrs Talbot about Trevor's behaviour; I think she was concerned in case he had given her any hassle. She said that up until the previous afternoon she had seen very little of Trevor, except for when he had called for his meals. She had seen a few of his friends arrive yesterday but she listened out and it didn't get too rowdy so she left well alone. When she got back from next-door she was reasonably convinced that his behaviour hadn't been too bad. Jack continued to moan though and threatened to, "sort him out"!

"He's just a teenager Jack, let it go."

"He's a bloody idiot, that's what he is."

"Weren't you his age once Jack?"

"Course I bloody was but my Dad would have thrashed me if I'd have done this."

"There's no real harm done; I've got stains out before and the glasses were only cheap things, I can clean things up."

"Let that little git do it; he made the mess, he should do it, you shouldn't have to."

"Just forget it, I'll deal with it; the grass needs cutting, you go and do that and I'll have a go at this."

"Oh sod it! I've got no authority in this house, with these kids, you're too protective. I'm going down the bloody Jockey!"

He grabbed his coat, paced up the hall and slammed the

door behind him.

During the following week, I think it was the Thursday night, the coppers were at the house again. Mom knew immediately that it must be Trevor they were after, but he wasn't in. I heard them ask to have a word with his Dad but Jack, who was stood looking on, shouted, "I'm not his bloody Dad!" And again he stormed off, this time into the back garden.

Mom asked the Police in and sat them down in the living-room, asking them what the problem was this time.

"Trevor's been making a bit of a nuisance of himself again, Mrs White."

"What's he been up to now?" Mom asked.

"He's been causing a few problems in Croft Street."

"What sort of problems?"

"Him and his usual mates have been tormenting Mrs Allen."

"You mean Mrs Allen the OAP?"

"Yes! That Mrs Allen; she's at the end of her tether, so to speak."

"What have they done?"

"They've been cheeking her and she said that they've smashed the glass in her greenhouse! They were throwing stones she said, 'purposely to cause damage'."

"I'm very sorry, I'll speak with Mrs Allen and I'll give Trevor a good talking to."

"We're afraid that's not good enough; Mrs Allen says that she doesn't want us to take things any further but she does want compensating for the damage that's been done. We've spoken with the other parents and as we are now telling you, you need to find £30.00 each."

"Thirty pounds?"

"Yes Mrs White £30.00, and you should feel that you're very lucky that she has insisted that we don't press charges. But, we will check up to ensure that the money has been paid."

Mom was very apologetic: "I'll sort it out, I'm so sorry, and I'll get Trevor to go and apologise, and he can offer to do a bit of gardening for Mrs Allen as well. I don't know what he's thinking of upsetting anyone, let alone old ladies."

Needless to say that when Jack came back inside, and Mom told him what had happened, he went straight through the roof again. He wanted Trevor out; he couldn't see that at the moment, it didn't really matter where Trev was, the police would still come calling upon us. Worse still was that Mom did not have the sort of money that they were asking for and she asked Jack for a loan. Jack was adamant that he would not find the money for Trev's misdemeanours and refused outright, "They keep saying they're not my bloody kids and they're not; you pay it!"

Embarrassingly Mom had to go cap in hand to Mr Hullstone and of course he helped out and he also said that he would speak to Trevor. When Trevor came home he had another bawling out from Mom and he told her that he was sorry and that he would put things right between him and Mrs Allen.

That wasn't the end of this little episode though because that night; I have no idea what time it was, but I do know that I had already been to sleep, and was suddenly awakened by banging. It was coming from Trevor's bedroom and there were raised voices; Jack's and Trevor's. I had no idea how long it had been going on, but I jumped out of bed and opened the door slightly so that I could hear what they were saying. As I peered out, I not only heard, but saw, Trevor who, by now, was holding Shipley by the throat, pinning him up against the wall. Shipley was obviously stoned; he was slurring his words and his arms were flailing frantically. Trevor was calling Shipley all sorts of things and I watched this long enough to see Trevor push Shipley full length upon his face, back into Mom's bedroom. As he turned back towards me; I could see that his lip was bleeding. I opened the door a little bit more and Trevor saw me; he snatched at the door handle and slammed it back in my face. He didn't hurt me because I moved quickly enough; I just stood shocked behind the door. Everything went very quiet; I stood for a while and then sat back down on my bed just listening for fear of what might happen next. Eventually I must have just fallen back to sleep because the next thing I remember is that I was being awakened by Mom, shaking me and telling me to get up because it was time for school.

When I got downstairs, I didn't say anything but I looked around for Trevor; he was nowhere to be seen.

"Where's Trev, Mom?"

"Oh, he's gone!" was all that she replied.

Up till that moment I hadn't really caught a glance at Mom's face that morning but now I could see that her eyes were puffed up and red; she had obviously been crying. I plucked up the courage to ask, "What was the rumpus about in the night, Mom?

"Come on, you'll be late for school," was all that she replied.

"What was going on with Trevor?" I asked again.

"Nothing!" she said angrily. "Don't ask any more questions!"

Pearl never spoke a word during these exchanges and now she just stood there obviously anxious to get off to school. Mom grabbed my things, put them upon the table, and actually took my cereal bowl from my hands.

"I hadn't finished yet Mom!"

"You'll be late! C'mon!"

Mom was obviously very upset and was definitely not her normal self; so I… grudgingly got up, snatched at my stuff and marched angrily down the hallway with Pearl following closely behind me. As I reached to turn the latch, Pearl tapped me upon my shoulder and said quietly, "Trevor's gone!"

All that day at school I couldn't concentrate. I just kept thinking about what Pearl had said. Trevor always came and went as he pleased now, didn't he? But I knew that she hadn't meant it in that way. I couldn't help but wonder if Trev would just be there as normal that evening, just ignoring everyone around him. I definitely hoped that he would be. I told Liam what had happened during the night and as usual, he was sorry about the way things were at home. He thought that perhaps Trevor would be there and that everything would be hushed up; things happened like that sometimes, didn't they? I told Liam that Shipley was ruining all of our lives and that I could see that deep down Mom wasn't really happy; well not like she'd been before. Liam suggested that I should just keep away from Shipley and that it might be best to avoid arguments and he said that he would explain everything to his Dad. I didn't know what his Dad could do; when I spoke with Liam, I didn't really understand what he could possibly do, but I had to speak to someone!

CHAPTER EIGHT

Trevor Goes The Wrong Way!

It had been almost a week now and Trevor had not been in touch with any of his family; he'd had enough of Shipley and knew that if he'd stayed any longer he'd probably have killed him.

***

"What you smoking, it stinks?"

"Here try some!"

"No thanks, what is it?"

"Just try it, you'll love it!"

"No! It's drugs innit?"

Corey just laughed, took one long puff, held it in for a few moments, and then he let the smoke drift slowly out from his nostrils and the corners of his closed mouth. His eyes were wide and he giggled a little stupidly.

Trevor said, "I'm bored, what we gonna do?"

"Don't know," slurred Corey.

"When's Lewis and Phil s'posed to be coming?"

"They'll be here! Why don't you cool it?"

Trevor wasn't really very happy where he was at this moment in his life but his options had diminished. 'Dossing' on Corey's sofa wasn't the best he could be doing with his life but circumstances had brought him here. He stood up and crossed the floor to gaze out through the window. What a dead-end hole; bins lying half-emptied of their contents upon the roadway; garage doors broken and smashed. Through one half of a damaged door he thought he could see movement, so he watched for a few moments. He knew that in that particular garage there was an old mattress lying on the floor. He could just make out three figures in there; it looked like two lads and a girl. Perhaps they were just mucking about? Trevor realised that his head was a little 'woozy' and he had a sickly taste in his throat. He turned to look back across the room to where Corey was. He was lying stretched out upon the filthy, old armchair; his legs were straddled wide open and his arms hung loosely alongside the chair. Trevor realised that he had nodded off. He crossed the floor and bent down at Corey's side, carefully removing the burning butt-end from his filthy fingers.

Trevor crossed back to the window carrying the butt with him, and stood once more for a brief moment, just gazing across the dirty road. It was now that he realised what the lads were up to. He could see that one of them was on the mattress with the girl and the other one seemed to be kneeling alongside them, appearing to be watching the action. Trevor looked down at the smoking butt in his fingers and glanced back across at Corey. He was still flat-out; well zonked. Trevor lifted the butt to his lips and drew on it. This was the first time; he spluttered and coughed. It was sweet tasting and the back of his throat began to tingle. He tried it once more and immediately began to splutter and cough again. What was he doing with his life? This thought entered his mind, but his thoughts were quickly diverted back across the road. Look at those 'dirty gets', he thought to himself. They could be catching all sorts. He lifted the latch on the window and cracked it open; it was not easy as it obviously hadn't been opened for some time. He rubbed the butt-end out upon the metal of the casement latch and then dropped it out of the window onto the dirt. Suddenly he realised that he was about to vomit. He rushed immediately into the kitchen, making it just in time to empty the contents of his stomach out into the stainless steel sink. These contents did not amount to much and he heaved painfully for the second time but nothing happened. He turned on the cold tap and slowly he watched the vomit dribble away down through the plughole.

As he stood there watching the last of it disappear, he heard the front door creaking open; footsteps, and then the living room door was pushed ajar.

"What you up to?" asked Lewis, seeing Trev bending over the sink.

Trevor turned to see Phil following Lewis through the door.

"Nothing!" he replied.

"What's up with him again?" asked Phil, referring to the state Corey was in.

"No need to ask, have you?" replied Trevor.

Lewis looked around at the state of the place. "Ain't this a doss-hole!" he said.

"No need to ask that either, have you?"

"I weren't asking, I was saying."

They all laughed aloud.

"What you doing at the sink anyway, you ain't washing up are ya?"

"Nah, I just threw up."

"Too much pop, eh? Where you hiding it then?" asked Phil.

"We ain't got no pop, but I just finished off his ciggy."

"Who, you?" Phil asked.

"Yeh, me first and the last!"

All three of them laughed loudly once more, and Trevor walked through to join them in the living room.

"Have you seen them dirty gets, over there?"

"Over where?"

"Over in that garage, look." He moved back towards the window and the other two joined him there. He pointed, "See in that one, look." Both of them stood there for a moment and then Lewis said,

"Wowee! He's going some!"

Trevor looked and then he realised that 'he' was now the previous onlooker, the lad on his knees.

"They've changed over," he said.

"What, they're both at it?" enquired Lewis.

"Yeh, certainly seems so."

"Dirty gets!" replied Phil.

Lewis asked, "Have you seen the girl, who is she?"

"No, I ain't seen any of them properly, you can't can ya? I don't really want to know either."

After standing for a while watching and listening to the occasional moans and groans from Corey they turned their attentions back inwards.

"I thought we were off out?" Lewis asked.

"Yeah, that's what I thought," said Trevor.

Phil had a kick at Corey's ankle and he grumbled loudly.

"Get up you idle get!" said Phil, and Corey grumbled again.

Lewis disappeared into the kitchen and then returned carrying a dirty mug; he slung its contents into Corey's face.

"What, what, what?" spluttered Corey, his eyes opening like saucers.

"Bloody shit!" he shouted. "You stupid get, what ya done that for?" His words were slurred but distinguishable.

"We ain't come here to watch you catch bloody flies!" moaned Phil.

Corey leaped from his seat and wrestled Phil to the

floor but Lewis and Trevor immediately pulled them apart. Corey and Phil just lay there on their backs, laughing.

When the four of them had finally sorted themselves out, Phil suggested that they should go down to the, 'offy', by the Park and get a few, 'Lightnings'.

"I ain't got no dough, Phil," said Corey.

"You've never got no dough!" said Lewis.

Phil said, "I'm flush, I had the 'gee-gees' come in."

"How much d'ya win then Phil?" asked Corey.

"Mind it! I got a few bob for Lightning, that's all you need to know."

So they all sauntered off out of the flat; Phil taking a great deal of interest in the garage opposite as they passed by, but it was now deserted. When they reached the off-license there were a few people waiting, so two of them sat on the park wall opposite, while Phil and Corey went and joined the queue. On the way down the aisle they grabbed two big bottles of Lightning and four bags of cheese and onion crisps. When they got to the counter it was old Atmar Singh who was serving; the Granddad of the Singh family. He was a bit on the slow side and very deliberate in all of his movements. It was obvious to Phil that Atmar did not like Corey by the disapproving looks that he was giving to him. When Phil handed over his cash, Corey was half-leaning across the counter, sort of slouching, probably still the after-effects of the drug. Phil took his change and then pushed Corey on the shoulder.

"Come on Coz!" he prompted.

There were still people queuing behind them and they had to move to one side to let them pass by.

They left the shop and crossed the road to the other two lads who immediately jumped down from the wall and followed behind them through a gap in the hawthorn hedge. The gate was another ten metres or so further on so this was a quicker route. When they got through and out onto the grass, Phil noticed that Corey was eating a Mars bar.

"Where'd ya get that from?" he asked.

Corey just winked at him and carried on chomping.

"Tea-leaf!" Lewis said, but Corey just grinned stupidly.

They crossed the field to their usual spot, on the slope, overlooking the duck pond. As soon as they'd all settled down, they started to pass the bottles backwards and forwards between them, taking large swigs whilst nibbling on their crisps.

"Did ya see the wads in that till?" Corey asked.

"What wads?" Trevor enquired.

"In old Singhy's till!"

"You couldn't help but see 'em, your head was half in there," said Phil.

"There must have been thousands!" replied Corey.

"There probably was," said Lewis. "He's always very busy in there."

It went quiet for a few moments and then with his mouth half-filled with crisps, Corey said, "We could take that!"

"What?" asked Lewis.

"Keep up!" said Corey. "I thought you was the one with the brains?"

"Count me out!" said Trevor.

"Out of what?" asked Phil.

"Bloody hell! What you lot on, I thought that it was only me on the weed?"

"I ain't getting into another robbery!" Trevor reiterated.

This line of conversation proceeded for a while and all this time the lads were knocking back the Lightning.

Phil eventually stood up and said, "Come on, I got enough readies, let's get some more."

Trevor said, "I'll come with yer."

But Corey struggled to his feet and said, "No! I'm going, you sit there softie."

Trevor did not take kindly to being spoken to in this way and Corey was beginning to bug him. Lewis must have recognised this in Trevor's face and he grasped at Trevor's forearm.

"Leave it Trev, he's out of it, just ignore it," Lewis said.

Phil and Corey walked away and after a few moments Trevor said, "He's gonna do for us!"

"How d'ya mean, 'do for us'?"

"We're all gonna end up in clankers, if we listen to that turd."

"I thought that you and him were mates?"

"Mates?"

"Yeah, he's given you a roof over your head ain't he?"

"I got no other offers, have I?" asked Trevor.

It all went quiet again until Lewis started to ask Trevor if he'd considered going back home again.

"I ain't got no bloody home any longer; not while he's got breath in his body!"

"Is he really that bad?"

"No, he's a damn site worse than I could ever say, I'll swing for him one day, I know that, I swear it!"

The other two lads returned with two more Lightning and four more bags of crisps. Then the banter quickly recommenced.

"You gonna be chicken then, Mommy's boy?" Corey suddenly taunted once more.

Trevor leaped at him, grabbing him by the collar and yanking his head backwards, down upon the grass.

"I ain't no bloody Mommy's boy!" he yelled. "I'll rip your bloody face off if yer keep it up!"

Phil caught hold of Trevor and screamed out, "Calm it

lads!"

Trevor let go of Corey and brushed Phil to one side.

Corey sat up, ruffled, and repeated the words, "It's full to bursting!"

"Don't have any more then, especially if you're gonna keep being stupid," said Lewis.

"Not me, you bloody idiot! The till Is!"

"Is it?" Lewis asked Phil, suddenly taking an interest.

Phil replied, "Yeah, I saw it, he's got twenties rolled up in elastic bands and he's putting some under the tray as well, I watched him."

All the while the others were chatting, Trevor had his hands firmly around the one Lightning; he was fired-up by Corey's taunts and was knocking back more than his fair share. After throwing up earlier and still having the after effects of the ciggy; he felt unusually light-headed and groggy. He suddenly shot up and threw his empty bottle into the air, and it splashed down into the pool.

"Come on then, what we waiting for?"

Lewis stared at him as if he was suddenly deranged.

"Are you bloody nutty?" he asked.

"No, I ain't, he thinks I'm bloody chicken, and I ain't!"

"You bloody idiot, he's only joking!" replied Lewis.

"Joking about what?" Corey asked, as if he had suddenly become resident upon another planet. Then he asked, "Joking about what, him being chicken or us doing Singhy?"

"About both!" shouted Lewis, getting very angry with this stupidity.

Trevor stood there kicking at the grass.

"I ain't joking about either," said Corey.

"I'm the only one of us stood up here!" snorted Trevor. "Your mouth's bigger than the rest of you Corey!" he snapped.

Corey struggled once more to his feet, and said, "I'm ready!"

Phil and Lewis looked at each other, as though they were asking, 'what the hell's going on here?' but neither of them spoke, they just got to their feet too, and all four of them headed back towards the gap in the hedge.

As they reached it Lewis said, "This is bloody stupid, there's too many, they're in and out all the while!"

Corey asked, "You chicken too?"

Lewis did not answer he just followed on behind the others as they crossed the street heading directly for the off-license.

As they reached the shop Lewis again pleaded, "Look, at least let's try and keep our senses, wait for a chance, eh?"

They bunched together on the pavement as if in discussion and Corey waited for the right moment. An old, grey-haired fellow left the shop and for a brief moment 'Singhy' was alone. Corey said to Lewis, "You get the door, okay?"

Lewis just nodded and all four entered together. Corey and Trevor approached the counter and Lewis dropped the latch on the door and reversed the sign to display, 'closed'. A woman approached the door and rattled the catch; Lewis turned his back on her. Phil stood between the shelves holding back in case of trouble. Corey offered two Mars bars over the counter from an adjacent shelf; Trevor stood alongside him. Mr Singh took the chocolate from Corey's hand and beeped the barcode. The till shot open revealing its packed contents and Corey grabbed Singhy by the wrist. Mr Singh pulled sharply away and Corey scaled the counter.

"Get the bloody money!" he cried out at Trevor.

Corey and Mr Singh both fell backwards into the sweet jars and they all ended up on the floor. Trevor pulled out the tray of cash and Phil arrived at his side; they swiftly shoved bundles of notes into their pockets. Phil threw the tray to one side and they helped themselves to what lay beneath it in the drawer.

Back at the doorway two men and the woman stood waiting; one of them noticed what was going on and tried to force the door but Lewis leant against it. Young Singh came rushing down the stairs and through the door into the shop having heard the commotion. Phil had to wrestle him to the floor. The open doorway revealed the rear exit and Trevor beckoned Lewis towards it; they had to step across the two who struggled on the floor in the entrance to the serving counter. Phil landed a direct punch on the young Mr Singh and stunned him. He then struggled up and shouted to Corey to get the hell out. The other two snatched open the back door and encouraged the others to get out now. Phil stood there just long enough to see Corey get to his feet clutching a knife; as old Singhy grabbed at Corey's ankles he watched in shear disbelief, as Corey sliced Singhy along the length of his forearm and blood shot everywhere. Corey joined Phil as they both fell out into the street and followed their mates down the road. By the time one of the male shoppers had arrived at the rear doorway all four were racing down the street. Corey's shirt was sprayed with Mr Singh's blood; Phil looked back at him in anger. They were all four blocks away in the old warehouse area before any of them decided to pause. They were doubled-up, gasping for breath, when Lewis and Trevor saw the state of Corey.

"What the hell you done, you stupid get!" screamed Trevor.

"Where you cut?" asked Lewis.

Phil turned his head, looked at Corey and jumped upon him dragging him to the ground and beating him with his fists. The others had to pull him off. Corey lay there motionless, his face bleeding from Phil's vicious blows.

"He's killed Singhy!" Phil screeched. "He's knifed him, I saw him do it, there was blood everywhere!"

"C'mon let's leave him there," said Lewis.

Trevor said, "We can't do that, he'll blurt, he'll tell everyone we were with him."

Lewis replied, "They seen us anyway, we had a bloody audience, what the hell we done?"

Corey started to gurgle noisily and they dragged him to his feet thinking that he might choke on his own blood. He stood there supported; head hung and blood running from his mouth.

"Let's get out of here," Phil said.

Lewis and Trevor dragged Corey along with them, his toes scraping the ground. They heard sirens in the distance but they were travelling away from them. Phil decided that it might be best if they all returned to his place for a few days; he didn't think anyone could have seen his face because he was turned away from the window. There was no better suggestion; the coppers knew the lads hung around together anyway but there was nowhere else to go.

There proved to be no hiding place because later that same evening the police arrived at Phil's and whisked the four of them away without even a tussle! Once again, the White's were informed of Trevor's latest stupidity and Mrs White knew that she could not prevent the surety of what would follow. She had just a brief period of contact with Trevor and was distressed, to say the least, to find her eldest son in such a state. She asked why, and he replied,

"Oh Mom, do you need to ask, life's a bloody mess, ain't it?"

It was devastating for Josh and Pearl; in disbelief they had to listen to the horror story of that day's events repeated many times over. Now Josh had truly lost his brother; he believed, for good. Shipley hadn't a care in the world; it was good riddance to bad rubbish as far as he was concerned. Josh couldn't help thinking that, if only this had been Shipley taken from the family instead of his brother, then all might be well!

Trevor now being gone long-term did not help at home. Shipley had his feet under the table and he became obsessed with his new-found supremacy. He was a nasty, cruel bully! He found it great fun to order them about; to criticise them and to spill out endless verbal psychological abuse, particularly away from Mother's ears. Pearl was the target for more of his nasty snide remarks than any other. The first time she brought a boy to the door he told him where to go! He criticised every choice of clothing that she ever made. He made remarks about her weight, her hair and her acne! In fact he seemed endlessly to be on her back about the triviality of everything in her life. All of this led to the increased confrontation between Josh and him. Josh, four years Pearl's junior, could not stand back and watch his sister destroyed in this manner. He increasingly noticed every jibe and offensive remark that was made and he bided his time.

CHAPTER NINE
Precious Pearl

I don't really know what it was that had caused me to wake from my deep sleep. It was very unusual for me because, since I had been set up in the little box-room, I only needed my head to hit the pillow; the next thing I'd know was that Mom would be calling me to hurry up! I always slept with my bedroom curtain partly open; leaving a wide gap in the middle, allowing whatever light there was to come through. On this occasion there was very little light; I lay there just a short while and I heard a sort of a whining sound. I tried to distinguish what it was. Cats in the garden sometimes made this sort of noise when they were squaring up to one another. I listened again carefully; it could also be foxes. I remembered on one occasion there was a fox behind our shed that made such terrible noises and I had had to fetch Dad out of bed. He reassured me of what it was; in fact we both sat in the bedroom window until we eventually saw the fox emerge and scale the back fence. There it was again; so I sat up in bed, rubbing my eyes. The noise was not coming from outside of the house at all; it was outside my bedroom door somewhere. I swung my legs out of bed and sat there.

Things where now very quiet and I wondered if or not I should just cover myself back up and forget it. There was a cry; it was definitely a cry. For a long time now I had been sleeping with the dresser in my room pushed against the door, so I pulled the dresser gradually away, but I was very hesitant, being unaware of what might happen next. My heart was beating rapidly and I steadied myself before slowly pushing open the door; it had a tendency to creak and I wanted to avoid this happening.

Nothing but a dark, quiet landing confronted me but I could hear low voices, mumblings. I had no slippers or socks on my feet and made no sound as I ventured outwards towards Pearl's door. Both Mom's bedroom door and Pearls were always left slightly open at night; there was no light on and just the moonlight lit between the shadows. I stood outside of Pearl's door and listened intensely. Shipley was accusing Pearl of having taken money from his wallet. He was obviously stoned out of his brain and didn't know what he was saying. He'd probably been on the Bell's again! I knew that Pearl would never have stolen from anyone. Shipley was just off his head again as he had been many times recently, and of late Pearl had taken most of his aggression. I wanted to swing open the door and blurt out, 'what the hell's going on here?' But, I couldn't! I was ashamed of myself. I thought, 'he'll leave her alone in a minute, he doesn't know what he's doing. Then there was a sudden creaking! I backed off and slid behind the cover of my own door; it was ajar enough just to be able to see Pearl's door open quietly and Jack's face appear. He didn't pause; he just quickly slid back into the other bedroom.

I stood behind my door in the shadows for at least fifteen minutes. My feet were like ice and I was shaking! I heard just for a brief while after his departure the dying sounds of that whimper from Pearl but then all had returned to normality. I slid my dresser back into place; I had no idea what the time was. I heard the sound of a police car in the distance lasting only a few moments, but nothing else. I slid back into bed and lay there dithering and slowly regaining normality. Then I was woken up by Mom, insisting that I should come down now or definitely be late. I hadn't heard anyone else before this. I knew that if I was going to be late then Jack must already have gone to work and that Pearl must already be waiting to head off to work; she was always ready before I was. I slipped once more from the warmth of my bedding and hurriedly dressed for school. When I got down to the foot of the stairs I was afraid to push open the door; I just didn't know what would confront me, but I heard Mom speaking quite normally with Pearl. I went in and Pearl was sitting there waiting. The radio was on and Mom started to hurry me along, pushing cereal in front of me and throwing my school stuff hurriedly together upon the sofa.

I sat there choking on my cereal. Pearl's eyes were red, she had definitely been crying. Neither Pearl nor Mom mentioned the incident in the night. I was determined to speak to Pearl about it; the whole episode had definitely not been a bad dream. I told Mom that I couldn't finish things; that I wasn't hungry, that I needed to hurry because we had Turley first lesson, and that he was a drama queen. I just wanted to get out of that house! Pearl and I walked silently up one road after another. She walked along with me on my way to school which meant that she would arrive at her job at Woolworths at about 8.45am which she reckoned was perfect timing. I didn't need an escort but I think that she just liked the early morning walk into town rather than sitting on a crowded bus. She was silent and so was I. This was not what I wanted; I needed to talk to her.

"Have you been crying?" I suddenly managed to blurt out.

"No!" she replied.

"Yes you have, I can tell."

"Shut up, you don't know anything!"

We went quiet again. We were only a short distance from the school and I wanted to cry too. I needed to talk to Pearl.

"You have been crying, haven't you! What for?"

"Oh Josh, it doesn't matter, don't make a fuss, nothing matters anymore."

"Of course it does, I don't know what you mean, 'nothing matters'?"

"Please Josh, don't make a fuss, you'll only make it all worse."

I looked at her, she had tears in her eyes and I must have had in mine because she brushed one to one side and gave me a reassuring look.

"I'm sorry," I said.

"You have nothing to be sorry for Josh, I love you."

I felt another tear come to my eye and I said, "I love you too."

She touched me upon my shoulder and we parted company going our different ways, and I arrived at school with time to spare. I couldn't help but go over those last few words in my mind. She had said that she loved me and I too had repeated the same words. I didn't recall either of us having said those words to each other for years. Perhaps it was our ages; perhaps we were both growing up. I knew that Pearl was very unhappy and I knew that I had let her down; I felt unwell, I couldn't concentrate, teachers kept shouting at me and telling me to get my mind on my work.

Liam asked me during the break what was wrong with me but I couldn't tell him; I couldn't tell anyone, but I knew when I got home that I was going to ask Mom what was going on. Liam and I did not leave the school together as we had to go our separate ways; anyway this would have been difficult because we tended to leave at different times. For one, I often had detention and Liam didn't, and for another, I sometimes hung around with the lads kicking a ball or for footy training or something. I knew that it was half-day at Woolies but Pearl was not at home when I arrived and I was late.

"Where's Pearl, Mom?"

"Wasn't she going to the library?"

"I don't know!"

"I think that's what she said; you were in too much hurry to listen. What was the matter with you this morning?"

"Didn't you notice that Pearl had been crying Mom?"

"No! She had got something in her eye, off the towel she said. She hadn't been crying!"

"She had Mom; you don't seem to care enough to notice now Mom!"

"Oh Josh, don't start all that stupid stuff again, we have a short while without it and then you have to stir things up!"

It went quiet for a few moments; Mom stuffed a banana in my hands.

"She had been crying Mom. Pearl and I both said that we loved one another this morning Mom. Do you still love us?"

"Oh, shut up Josh! You're doing my head in, what is the matter with you? If this is leading to another big argument about Jack, then I don't want to know!"

I got very angry and shouted, "No you never bloody do! You haven't answered my question, do you love us?"

"You can watch your language for a start, there's no calling for language. What are you getting so worked up about anyway?"

The door opened and Pearl walked in. She asked, "Why are you two shouting? I could hear you outside."

I went up to my bedroom; it occurred to me that I was becoming Trevor. Whenever there was no resolution to a situation the answer was to hide in my bedroom. That wasn't the end of it though. Mom had not said that she loved us and I knew that Shipley was accusing Pearl for something that she would never have done, and that could not continue. But for now, I hid in my bedroom.

It was about three days later into that week that I walked in to witness another confrontation between Pearl and Shipley. He wasn't drunk this time but he didn't need to be to behave obnoxiously; I'd found this out. Pearl was giving it back to Shipley as good as she was able, but he was red-faced and aggressive. I just blew it; I couldn't hold it any longer, so I squared up to him and confronted him.

"Do you know that you're a right pain in the butt!" and I threatened, "If you don't lay off my sister once and for all then I'll kill you!"

I was naive, foolish and unworldly! I didn't know men like Shipley; I thought they existed only in films! I was standing too close to him and without hint or warning he swung about and kicked me hard between the legs and I fell to my knees in agony! He sneered at me. "Tell your Mommy about that one, but don't forget that you'll have to show her to prove it!"

Pearl jumped at him; she hung around his neck and clawed at his face with her nails until he callously forced her grip away from him and punched her straight in the mouth! She reeled about with her hands clasped to her face and hung across the sink with blood dripping from between her fingers. Shipley spluttered out, "Now bloody grow up the pair of yer and pull your weight!" before he left through the rear door slamming it viciously behind him!

I met Mom, as she approached from work, halfway down our street. She looked very angry and started shouting before I got the chance to open my mouth. I just couldn't believe it! Shipley had got to her first and according to his version of events he had broken up a fight between Pearl and me! Mom ranted on about all of us disrespecting her and her relationship! She accused us of never giving Shipley a fair chance! I tried several times to get a word in edgeways but she was having none of it; I just let her go ranting on in front of me. I went and sat upon the garden wall, numbed and in disbelief. Mom was blind as far as Shipley was concerned and it seemed that no matter what happened, we came second! I thought that when Pearl had the chance to explain the events to Mom that she would have to believe us, but she didn't!

Poor Pearl, she looked at me in desperation. Her mouth was swollen and Mom yelled at me for hitting a girl! I screamed out, "Don't you realise that you're behaving like a bloody fool; Shipley has tied you around his little finger!"

I reminded her about the blonde in the house and she screamed and smashed a plate against the kitchen wall. I was about to reel around and head once more for my room, when she demanded that I go there anyway! I screamed back, "Oh don't you worry that's where I was going, I can't bear to be near you for a second longer!"

I kicked the kitchen door and slammed the hallway door behind me! Pearl came to my room shortly after; she was in tears and she said, "Mom's crying down there."

I told her, "I don't want to know about Mom!" And then I asked, "Are you okay?"

She sat on my bed and held her head in her hands so I sat beside her with my arm about her shoulders. She was distressed and just as I needed Mom so did Pearl. I decided to go and fetch a cold wet flannel for her bruised mouth. Pearl had tried to help me and she had come off worse than I had. She held the flannel to her mouth for just a few moments and then asked if I was okay; and I told her that I was. I said that Shipley would pay for his actions. We just sat there for the next hour; talking about the stupid position that we now found ourselves in, before going to bed. I lay awake in bed just thinking about what had happened that day and wondering why Mom had now become the person she was. Mom, well she never even came to see how we were!

CHAPTER TEN

Late Night Fishing

"Can I go then Mom?"

"No, I've told you, you have to wait for your Dad!"

"He can come to me, can't he?"

"No! I don't like you going on your own."

"How long did he say he'd be then?"

"He didn't, he just said that the Boss had asked him to stay on a bit but he'd get away as quick as he could."

"But you don't know how long?"

"Liam, I've told you I don't know now stop keep pestering me, I've got a lousy head and now this damn washing machines sticking again."

Liam had been sitting in the living room, shouting through to his Mom. He and his Dad's fishing gear was all piled in the hall waiting for the off. He kept jumping up and down and looking for the first sighting of his Dad through the window. He walked through into the kitchen.

"What is it, Mom?"

"It's this bloody thing again; the knob's sticking!"

"I thought Dad had done it once?"

"He has, but it's started again now."

Liam showed an interest; he was getting older and more inquisitive about these sorts of things. He very often watched his Dad repair stuff and often held or passed things to him. He grasped at the knob.

"It seems alright Mom."

"No it ain't, it's stuck!"

"What d'yer mean stuck?"

"It's got to that point now where it ain't moving any further!"

"Oh!" Liam pushed it in, pulled it out and tried to spin it. He repeated it again but still it didn't move.

"Liam leave it; you don't know what yer doing and I don't want to make it any worse, Dad'll be here soon."

Liam stood up and walked back into the living room; he looked again through the window and there was still no sign of his Dad. Then he heard his Mom shout, "Oh bloody hell, the thing's come off now!"

He went back through.

"How'd yer do that?"

"I don't know; I just pulled the thing."

"You'll have to leave it to Dad, Mom stop messing! Mom can I go; there's still no sign of Dad and…well, please can I go?"

By now Mrs Hullstone had had just about enough. She was exasperated from her efforts and her head was aching.

"Oh go; I'll tell Dad to come straight to you when he gets in, this'll have to wait!"

Liam kissed his Mom, ran into the hall, gathered up his stuff and shot out through the door.

He kept an eye open for his Dad all the way down their road but once he had reached Poole Lane he knew that he was off his Dad's normal route home. He passed no one at all and the first voice he heard seemed to come out of nowhere. "Going fishing Liam?"

He looked around but saw no one.

"Liam!" The voice shouted louder.

He looked around and saw, across the lane, Jimmy Rogers, a mate from school, in his bedroom window, "Oh it's you Jimmy, I couldn't see yer!"

"You off fishing?" Jimmy asked again.

"Yeah course I am, I got me stuff ain't I?"

Jimmy shouted, "I might see ya later!" and then shut the window.

Liam walked along then turned left into Watery Lane. Here the houses started to thin out until there were huge gaps of rough land between them. At the end of the lane he climbed the small slope and up onto the canal side. Not a single person was to be seen in either direction. He walked along to their normal place where he knew his Dad would come to him; he did not expect him to be too long.

He sat there for about ten minutes or so on his basket, with his gear spread out beside him, and his rod in his hand. He noticed a figure getting closer to him and there was a little dog running in front. He thought to himself, it's Mrs Hammond and Bertie, and sure enough it was. She always stopped to speak to Mr Hullstone and Liam, and Bertie had grown used to Liam over the years. As he approached he shook from nose to tail and slid down onto his stomach, back legs full stretch. Liam stroked him behind the ear and he rose up, pushed himself nearer and dropped again.

"Where's yer Dad, son?"

"Oh he's late at work."

"Had yer ought to be on yer own?"

"Yeah, I'm alright, thank you Mrs Hammond."

"Is yer Dad coming to yer?"

"Yes he is, he won't be long."

"Yer take care lad it's awfully quiet."

Liam patted Bertie on his rear and he jumped up and trotted after Mrs Hammond. After about thirty minutes Liam still hadn't had a single tickle on his float and his Dad had still not arrived. He looked about anxiously and decided to move further on down in the direction of the little footbridge and the locks to try to change his luck.

He settled down again for another five minutes or so until he saw a bike coming towards him from the direction he had moved in. He looked on and suddenly realised that it was Jack Shipley. Jack pulled his bike up alongside him. Liam felt the hatred swell up inside of him and his heart pounded. This was the first time that their paths had crossed since Josh had told him about how he had kicked him.

When he'd heard, he was mad, really very mad indeed. He insisted that Josh tell the police. He asked what Josh's Mom was going to do about it. He told him that he'd tell his Dad, but to every suggestion Josh had insisted that he said nothing. With brave and angry words he'd said that he would kill him if he ever touched him again.

"What d'yer want?"

"Nothing son, just being friendly."

Shipley stood down from his bike and leant it against the hedge. Knowing now what he did about Shipley he found himself spluttering out nervously, "My Dad'll be here in a minute."

"Oh, I was going to ask you where he was."

"He'll be here in a minute."

"What's the matter son, you alright?"

Liam stood up; he didn't like the way that Shipley was towering over him and he wanted him to see that he was not just a little kid. He shook, and was afraid that Shipley would see this, but his anger caused him to speak out.

"I know about Josh; you leave him alone you nasty get, because I'll say something if he don't!"

Shipley appeared to be taken aback. His face whitened and then he grabbed Liam by the shoulder.

"I don't know what Josh has told yer but he's an idiot; you keep yerself to yerself! I'm warning yer, keep your little mouth shut tight!" At this point he squeezed Liam roughly by the jaw, clambered back onto his bike, and pedalled off down the canal.

Liam's face hurt him; he was shaking after the encounter and thought about moving on, gathering his stuff up quickly and going home, but then he thought, why should I? It was all quiet again and the birds were whistling. Five lonely minutes passed by and then he saw Mrs Hammond coming back towards him, and Bertie came dashing to his side. Perhaps he should tell her just in case. He thought, 'no I can't, what would I say?' Mrs Hammond stood back alongside him.

"Yer still on yer own then son?"

"Yes Mrs Hammond, I'm alright."

"Are yer sure son?"

"Yes Mrs Hammond."

She leaned towards him, looking into his face.

"What's that yer got on yer lip son?"

Liam brushed his lip with the back of his hand. He looked and there was a little blot of blood on it.

"Oh," he said, "I just caught myself with my rod Mrs Hammond, I didn't know I'd done that."

She reached in her handbag and pulled out a tissue.

"Here use this, are you sure yer alright and yer Dad's coming?"

"Yes Mrs Hammond, I'm sure."

"Take more care with that rod, we don't want you spoiling such a pretty little face, do we? Come on Bertie."

Off they went once more leaving Liam in the silence. He was getting fed up but then his float dipped and he snatched at the line. He teased the fish in until it left the water; it was a roach, not too big but something to show his Dad when he got there.

Meanwhile Shipley had pedalled off down the canal-side like a madman his anger burning up within him. He swung his bike down and out onto the lane across the gravel slope causing bits to fly everywhere. In his mind he turned over the possibilities. If Josh had told Liam, then who else had he told?

***

Mr Hullstone was bending down in the kitchen, fiddling with the broken washer knob.

"Leave it until later, it'll wait."

"It shouldn't take long to put right."

"I know but leave it now; I'm worried about Liam, just please get down to him before it's too late, you could still get another hour before the light goes."

Mr Hullstone kissed his wife and gathered his gear from the hall where Liam had left it. She stood on the step and he waved to her as he reached the end of their road. When he got to the bottom end of Watery Lane he went up the small slope onto the canal towpath. He looked towards the right to the position where he expected to find Liam but he was not there. He looked towards the left and could not see him there either. He was a little disappointed that Liam had not stayed in the position that he had agreed to meet him. He thought for a moment and then decided that if anything, Liam would have moved closer towards the locks and the little footbridge. This spot had always been known for the bigger catches. So Mr Hullstone set off in that direction. There were very few twists or turns in this stretch and he became concerned that Liam was not in sight. At that moment he saw two people approaching from that direction so he stood there waiting for them.

"Hello, have you seen a lad fishing close by?"

"No, sorry."

"Have you seen anyone at all?"

"Not for a while."

"Okay, thank you."

Where could he be? Mr Hullstone returned slowly in the opposite direction. The canal took a sharper turn about a hundred metres on, so he decided to check around that bend, just in case. As he approached the bend he was hoping that he would see Liam's happy smiling face coming to greet him, having been told by the passersby that someone was looking for him. He was ready to give Liam a telling off for having moved away and caused him so much concern; but Liam did not turn the corner, and when Mr Hullstone had that full stretch of canal in his sight, all he could see was the departing figures of those strangers. Needless to say, Mr Hullstone became very anxious and he began shouting Liam's name but there was no response. He walked up by the locks and crossed the little footbridge but everywhere was quiet. Mr Hullstone decided to return home immediately having decided that he had missed Liam on the journey there, or that perhaps Liam had got fed up waiting and gone off with a friend. He expected that he would find him at home and that all would be well.

When he got home Mrs Hullstone heard his approach and said, "You back already? I've fixed it myself, you needn't have rushed, it just pushed back onto the spindle."

Mr Hullstone pushed open the door and asked, with concern in his voice, "Is Liam home?"

"No why, isn't he with you?"

"I can't find him, he wasn't there!"

"Well where could he be? He said to tell you he'd be in the same place."

"He wasn't there, I checked along both sides of the

canal."

"Perhaps he met a friend?"

"That's what I thought, but who?"

"Phone Josh he's the most obvious, isn't he?"

Mr Hullstone lifted up the telephone and rang the Whites' number; it just rang and rang and rang.

***

Liam was with Jimmy Rogers in his house. They were playing with a new game that Jimmy had had for his birthday the week before; he had told Liam about it at school. Jimmy had spotted Liam returning from the canal-side; Liam had been walking slowly up the street, still concerned about Shipley's threats towards him. He'd called him over and asked if he wanted to see the blow-football game that he'd had. Liam did, and he had got so involved that he'd forgotten all about the time. Mrs Rogers' voice brought him back down to earth and he realised that she was shouting to remind him of how late it was getting. He quickly said goodbye and gathered up his fishing tackle from the hallway of Jimmy's house and then made a quick sprint back home.

When Liam walked through the back door of his house his Dad was furious and so was his Mom when she heard the furore. He tried to explain, and kept repeating how sorry he was until suddenly they calmed down and, in relief, his Mom put her arms around him. He didn't understand what all the fuss was about but his Dad told him how worried they had been and that he had searched for him on the canal-side and tried phoning people to find him. His Mom got him a hot drink and he told them all about Jimmy Rogers and his blow-football, but he never said a word about Shipley.

CHAPTER ELEVEN
The Black Void

Since we had had our big confrontation with Shipley, Pearl and I drew even closer and soon I began to fear that all was not well with her. There were more confrontations, not on the same scale but always nasty! Pearl took the brunt of it. By now we had realised that Mom could not be our ally because, well, because I don't really know, and I found it increasingly more and more difficult to comprehend. Pearl was losing weight; I watched her as she picked over her meals. For some time now Shipley had tormented her about firstly her curves and then slowly this had turned to overweight jibes. He had begun by rudely turning away her early boyfriends but now he taunted her over her lack of boyfriends. I told her that she was just seventeen and that she didn't need to be in a rush for boyfriends; they would be coming soon enough. I waited patiently, hoping that Mom would come to her senses and hoped that she too would notice that Pearl was so unhappy. The rift was wide; it seemed that it could not be breached. In avoiding confrontation Mom avoided her responsibilities and became, 'detached'.

I realised that Pearl was leaving the dining table after having taken only a few mouthfuls, having only turned the food over and over upon her plate. Then she would go straight upstairs to the toilet. Eventually I followed her and I sat upon the top-step of the stair listening to her heaving in the toilet! It was difficult to approach the subject; I was distressed to hear her and realised that Pearl might find me annoying if I questioned her about it. Eventually I just had to ask, "What's going on Pearl; I've noticed how you keep rushing off to the toilet halfway through your meals, I can see that you're not eating and I've heard you vomiting, are you okay?"

I remember Pearl standing on the landing looking very frail and white.

"I'm fine Josh, please don't make a fuss, will you?"

"I'm worried about you Pearl and I can see that Mom is not aware of your poor health."

"I'll be okay Josh so please don't say anything to Mom, will you?"

"Have you seen a doctor, Pearl?"

"No I haven't; it's just a stupid bug or something, I'll be fine Josh!"

Over the coming days, weeks and then months, I watched Pearl slowly getting thinner and weaker. I approached the subject several times but Pearl would start to cry and I felt sorry for pestering her so I began to lay off. In the whole of that period I never once heard Mom question her about her health. Shipley on the other hand had changed his taunts about her 'fatness' to her now being, "a bag of bones!" Mrs Hullstone asked Pearl if she was okay; she asked about what diet she was on and commented about her new slim looks. I don't know if it was just out of politeness but she too did not seem too concerned about Pearl's health. So I did eventually ask Mom if she thought Pearl was okay; I found it difficult to talk to Mom about anything then all she said was that it was just teenage girls' ways and that I didn't understand. She was right about that, I didn't! I knew that Pearl was not on a diet; I knew that she was hardly eating anything or keeping it down, and I knew that Pearl was not just losing weight. Pearl looked paler by the day; she was drawn in the face and appeared slower in mobility. When we walked in the early morning, Pearl seemed breathless at times. Eventually I discussed it with Mrs Hullstone because it was obvious that Mom's attention was elsewhere. She initially took exactly the same position as Mom had. She also believed that it was just a stage in Pearl's life and that I didn't understand. I told her that I thought it was something to do with the way Shipley constantly ribbed her about being overweight. Her reply was, "there you go then, she's probably got tired of it and wants to lose some just to show that she can!"

Mrs Hullstone had taken some convincing that there was anything deeper troubling Pearl but at least she listened, which was different to Mom. When she did speak with Pearl; after cleverly arranging a shopping trip between the two of them, Pearl apparently was adamant that she was fine and all was well! It was fortunate that Mrs Hullstone saw through Pearl; she knew her better and was persistent. I sat in the kitchen listening to Mrs Hullstone explaining to Mom that she too believed that Pearl was not well, and that she ought to see a Doctor. Mom told her that I'd discussed it with her before and she'd suggested that I should not have pestered her with such nonsense. Mrs Hullstone however, did not agree now that it was nonsense. I thought that I may hear their first quarrel but after a little heated discussion, Mom agreed to talk to Pearl.

We were all sat around the dinner table; Pearl, Mom and me. This was about twenty minutes after Pearl had arrived home from work. Shipley was regularly late these days; he'd told Mom that he was having to work later at his job. I sensed that the air was a bit tense; Mom was edging around things and I began to think that she was not going to say anything at all! Then suddenly out of the blue; "You're looking a bit peaky today Pearl, are you okay?"

"Yes I'm fine, Mom!"

"Are you sure; I've noticed that you're losing a lot of weight, aren't you, Pearl?"

Pearl looked across at me searchingly and I thought that, just for one moment, she was going to say something to me, but she didn't.

"I've been on a new diet, Mom, it's very good!" she said.

Mom replied, "You don't want to overdo it, you know Pearl, you're okay as you are, and you read such things these days, don't you?"

"I've already left it off, Mom. I'm no longer on it!"

Pearl stood as she finished this sentence and said, "Excuse me, I need the toilet!" And she hastily made for the door.

When Pearl had safely disappeared through the doorway, Mom said, "There you go, I told you Josh, everything's good!"

"No it's not Mom, did you really think that Pearl was just going to tell you outright that she has this huge problem?"

"Yes, why shouldn't she?"

"Oh Mom, bloody hell! Pearl is ill! She's probably being sick right now and she's hardly touched her food, has she?"

Mom stood up immediately and went into the hall; she was a few minutes before returning. She sat back down opposite me.

"I just stood at the bottom of the stairs listening; all I can hear is the tap running, she is probably just having a wash."

"Then why has she left her food to go and wash?"

"I don't know Josh, don't make everything sound so mysterious and complicated, perhaps as she said she just, 'needed the toilet urgently!'"

"Mom Pearl is ill! Please don't leave it at that, will you?"

Mom got up again; she seemed in a bit of a 'huff'! I heard her trudging up the stairs.

I sat there at the table, picking over what was left of my dinner. I was wondering what was going on and I was worried that Pearl was okay. After twenty minutes neither of them had reappeared so I started to clear the table and place the washing up into the sink. Mom had more or less finished off her meal but Pearl's plate was still half-full of what was now, very cold food. Shipley had still not arrived (for which I was grateful), so I washed the crocks and then went to listen in the hall. I could hear low voices and the occasional sobbing; it sounded as if Pearl had become upset! I went back into the living room and switched on the television; I couldn't concentrate on whatever it was that was on. I just waited anxiously for Mom to return. Eventually Mom did reappear on her own; her eyes were reddened, so she too had been crying. She just sat down without a word; so I asked, "Well?"

"She's not well, Josh! She was being sick so I put my arms around her shoulders to hold her because she looked so white!"

A tear rolled down Mom's cheek and she brushed it to one side with the back of her hand.

"I could feel every bone in her body Josh; she's a bag of bones!"

"What we going to do, Mom?"

"I don't know Josh, she can't even talk to me properly, and she just keeps crying!"

"Where is she now then Mom?"

"I helped her into bed Josh, she didn't even want to come back down. I don't know what I'm going to do with her!"

I wanted to go straight to Pearl, but somehow I couldn't. I just sat there with Mom; neither of us knowing what to say next. The silence was broken only when the back door swung open against the wall; Shipley was home! His first words were not, 'hello anyone home?' And they were not, 'hello, is everyone okay?' His first words were, "Where's my bloody dinner, I'm starving!"

Mom pressed my hand as she got up immediately in response.

"Hello, are you okay?" she asked.

"Where's my dinner!" he replied.

"It won't be a minute; I've been held up!" Mom answered.

I heard a bit of mumbling in response to that but I couldn't make out what was said. Then I heard Mom say, "Jack, you've been drinking again!"

"Bloody shut up, woman! Give a man some peace in his own house, won't ya!"

With that little outburst, I got up and went straight to my room. I barely caught sight of Jack as I crossed the living room. In this sort of mood I didn't want to be anywhere near him!

The following morning I watched Pearl carefully as she sat and ate about half a round of toast. She insisted that she was well and that she was definitely going to work. Mom tried to persuade her that that was not a good idea and that she would be better off at home, but Pearl did not listen! We left the house together and there was some unnerving silence between us initially, until she finally asked, "Have you been telling Mom and Mrs Hullstone about me, Josh?"

I took a moment to answer and then I replied, "Yes! I was worried about you."

"You're just making things worse, you know that, don't you?"

"Pearl, I'm sorry, but I don't think that I am. I think that you need some help and I don't know what to do, can't you see how concerned I am?"

Pearl was annoyed with me, I could tell, but the last thing that I had wanted to do was to upset her! She suddenly said, "I'm late! I have to hurry! Then she dashed off in front of me, leaving me in my tracks and a little bit stunned!

At school that day, for the first time, I began to notice just how friendly Liam had become with Jimmy Rogers. I'd never really been too aware of this before and I just thought that it must be the mood that I was in. We always had other pals at school, obviously – especially when we got together in the playground – there were usually seven or eight of us. But I noticed the whispering between Liam and Jimmy, and I overheard them arranging their next fishing trip together. I hadn't really realised that they were seeing one another outside of school. I asked Liam after, a little later that day, and he simply told me that, as I hadn't been around so much lately and because his Dad rarely brought him to my house now, he had started to go fishing with Jimmy and they sometimes just knocked about together. I never meant to give Liam the impression that I was upset about this, in any way whatsoever, but he must have sensed this and added, "we're still best mates!" as if to reassure me that I had nothing to worry about. Really, I knew that I had been too busy soaking up everything that was happening at home and that I hadn't realised that I hadn't been there for Liam! I'd taken all of my worries to him and he never once failed me, but since I'd lost my Dad, and mainly because of Jack, our families were drifting apart. It started me thinking about how often I had been with Liam recently, besides being at school, obviously. Over the last three months there had been very few occasions.

When Pearl arrived home from work she seemed a little

brighter; she was bubbly and talkative, but I noticed that her eyes still looked very distant. There were lots of things racing through my mind. 'Why had Trevor been so stupid and why had he never thought about his responsibilities towards the family?' I also returned to the old sour potato, 'why the hell had Mom ever got involved with Jack? I couldn't stop thinking about Pearl's condition; 'what if she were to die?' I realised that it would just be Mom, me and Jack. The thought was unbearable! Jack had, I realised, driven a wedge between our family! I hated him! It burned within me stronger than ever; Trevor was not there (because of Jack), Pearl, I decided, was ill (because of Jack) and Mom was a shadow of her former self (because she was completely obsessed with Jack!) Now to top it all, I believed that Liam had become distanced (because of Jack)! I was suddenly aware that Mom was trying to push a mug of tea into my hands, "What is up with you?" she asked.

I was a million miles away!

Over the next few weeks I kept a constant eye on Pearl and I was also aware that Mom was making a lot more effort too. I heard Mom talking to Jack about Pearl; she was telling him how concerned she was, but Jack seemed oblivious to either of us, unless of course he was in a foul mood or stoned and then we were the objects of his aggression! He was totally insensitive and he was also totally unaware of some of the tremendously awful gaffs that he would make. He never seemingly gave consideration to his choice of words! Having been made aware of Pearl's condition and the concerns that Mom had, he still insisted, on one day, to offer his words of wisdom on Pearl's choice of make-up, as if he knew anything! It was both offensive and annoying because he was suggesting that Pearl, had "No reason to look so pale because if she tried harder and with the right kind of make-up, she could soon put some colour back in her cheeks and a smile upon her face!" I suppose that I had, by now, become hyper-protective towards her and I clashed with Jack as soon as I heard his words. I told him that he was a stupid moron and just how crass he was! His words to me were, "Butt-out!"

Due to my awareness of Liam's friendship with Jimmy, I started to make a bigger effort to do more stuff with him. I even went rooting in the garage hoping to dig out my old bike, or Trevor's, because I thought I could ride over to his now and again, but the bikes had gone! I was very annoyed and when I asked Mom, she just said, "Oh Jack had a clear-out ages ago, you were never going to use them again, were you?" I was furious with Jack but also with Mom too for allowing the bikes to be thrown out without asking first!

I screamed at her that, she had "No right letting Jack chuck them out!" Of course it didn't help not having the bike, because it made things a lot more difficult, and Mom was adamant that no way could she afford to buy me a new one. Now I just couldn't get to Liam's in the way that I'd hoped. I started instead, to go home after school with Liam; his Dad had no problems with dropping me home a little later, but I was always conscious that I was not there for Mom and Pearl! It was actually on one of the occasions that Mr Hullstone was taking me home, that he pointed out Jack's car parked up in a side lane.

He asked, "Isn't that Jack's car parked down there?"

He gestured toward the car, which did look very familiar! It was parked away from the main thoroughfare, in a little woody side lane. I told Mr Hullstone that I couldn't quite make out the number plate but I was damn sure that it was his! I asked him, "Do you mind going down by it?"

He seemed a little reluctant but then he did, stopped, reversed back and drove down past it very slowly. As we passed by he said, "I think that we should leave well alone

Josh!"

Mr Hullstone knew well enough that I was old enough to understand what Jack was up to, and that I was no fool. I just replied, "Don't worry, I shan't get you involved!" But I wanted to be certain. And certain I was; we passed close enough for me to see clearly that Jack was leaning across the passenger seat and he appeared to be kissing a dark-haired woman! So it wasn't the blonde that I had seen at our house! The time that we had spotted them was after Jack's regular finishing time, so I figured that this must be the overtime that he was doing! Mr Hullstone said that I should consider Mom's feelings and reminded me how upset she would be. To me, it was another nail in Jack's coffin!

Mom saw me on the way up the path and she met me at the door just in time to wave Mr Hullstone off. He never hung about these days; that was, unless he was visiting with the others, but he usually timed that to Jack's known absence! Mom put my dinner out upon the table and I asked where Pearl was; Mom said that she had gone to have a lie down. I asked if she was alright and Mom said that she appeared to be but she was just a little tired. I started to eat my dinner and Mom sat with me; she had no real need to because she had eaten earlier, but this was something that she tended to do. I looked up at her but she was hidden behind her evening newspaper and I said, "Guess who we saw on the way home?"

Mom looked out above the paper and enquired, "I don't know Josh, who did you see?"

"Jack!"

"Jack, where did you see him?"

I hesitated and then said, "It don't really matter Mom, but he's not working overtime, well not in the office anyway!"

Mom looked at me inquisitively but I could see that

there was also a touch of anguish upon her face. She didn't say anything, so I continued, "Mr Hullstone spotted Jack's car, so we drove past it very slowly. Jack was all over this dark-haired woman."

Mom still said nothing; she just sat there looking a sorry figure. I did not want to hurt Mom but I believed that she deserved to know the truth!

Suddenly she stood up and folded her paper, put it under her arm, picked up her mug of tea and walked off into the front room. I heard the television suddenly start to blaze out. As soon as I'd finished eating I followed her through; she was just sitting there with the paper on her lap.

"I'm sorry Mom!" I said. She still said nothing.

I couldn't stand the silence so I asked, "You do believe me, don't you?"

I could now see that she had tears in her eyes and she replied, "Of course I believe you Josh."

I couldn't help but say, "Well you didn't believe me when I told you about the blonde, did you?"

"Yes, I did, Josh!" she said, looking me directly in the face and making me feel rebuked. Then she continued, "I love you Josh! I love all three of you, no matter what you think! I believed you then as I believe you now but I chose not to want to know! Can't you understand that Josh?"

Sadly I replied, "No Mom, I can't!"

For the first time in a long long while Mom got up, sat next to me and put her arms around my shoulders; she just sat there and cried. I felt awful, I didn't know how to cope, I hadn't got the words for her. I just sat there thinking, 'she said that she still loves us, all three of us!' I had a lump in my throat! I still could not speak. Mom eventually got up and went back into the kitchen; I could hear her washing crocks but I just could not move for a while. There was something on the television but I can't even remember what it was. When I finally had the courage to go to her, I found her laying the table ready for Jack's return, I was about to speak but I heard him approach the back door so I just shot off upstairs. I wanted to be well out of his way; I could not have looked him in the face without feeling the need to jump on him and choke him!

I went in and sat by Pearl's bed; she looked so tiny and delicate. She was asleep; her face was like porcelain and she had the appearance of a little doll! I was very tempted to hold her hand, it was resting so softly upon the white pillow. I didn't want to wake her; she looked at peace in herself, but it then occurred to me how dark she was around her eyes; I'd not really noticed this before. It was only seven o'clock but Pearl seemed to be sleeping more and more these days. I suddenly found myself feeling very tearful. I had left Mom downstairs, a victim of life, and I failed to see how life could possibly get itself into such a mess! I must have sat at Pearl's bedside for at least an hour; I could hear the occasional raised voice from down below. Unfortunately, to me, this was now the normal way of our household. I thought about Liam and what he had been telling me about his fishing trips and the fun that he had with his Dad; it also played on my mind that whilst I was stewing in my own torrid life, he was laughing and playing with Jimmy Rogers like any teenager should do. Knowing now that they went fishing together; just the two of them, either on the canal or the park pool, made me feel that our lives had become poles apart from each other! Liam was a good friend; he always had been and his parents were like a second family to me, but we saw a lot less of them all now. Even in school Liam and I had become separated by the set system. For the last few years I had accepted that I had been failing in my education whereas Liam had continued to succeed. He had got good results from tests and he did his homework regularly; I knew that I had let everything slip. It would not be long now before we left school and whilst Liam spoke of an apprenticeship, I only had the promise of a job that had been offered by my Uncle Fred at his warehouse!

I couldn't believe the normality of the house again the next morning. Pearl was getting ready for work as normal and Mom was in the kitchen scurrying about laying out the breakfast so that we were not late. On the way to school Pearl chatted about her work and my schooling but domestic life was not mentioned. She asked if I was looking forward to joining the workers because my time was drawing near. I just answered, "yes." I had no real enthusiasm either for or against it. In the break-time at school, I began to find out a little bit more about Liam's adventures. He was enthusiastic to tell me more; he started by saying that, he still wished that I could enjoy fishing as he did. I replied that even if I did, I don't think that I could spend that sort of time away from home because of the way things were! Liam replied sternly, "You can't carry the weight of the world upon your shoulders, Josh! No one person can! You have your life to live and, as Dad is always telling me, 'it'll be gone before you know it!'"

"It's Pearl and Mom! I feel responsible, especially because Trevor's no longer around!"

I could see by Liam's eyes that I had lit a fire beneath him and he sighed, "Oh mate! You're not responsible; you're only fifteen, you can't be responsible! Look Josh, please try to get out more, live your life, think about coming out with us, we have a laugh, please try!"

As I reached home that night, I was just turning into our path and Mrs Gould shouted at me from next-door. I went back to her to see what she wanted and, when I met her at the front doorway, she just ushered me in. I followed her up the hall, half expecting Mom to be there with her but when we got into the living room, she announced, "You're to have your dinner with me tonight, Josh!"

"But why?" I asked.

"Your Mom's been called away to the hospital, it was about three-ish; it seems that Pearl was taken poorly at work son!"

She walked in to the kitchen so I shut the middle door and followed her.

"What did they say had happened to Pearl, Mrs Gould?"

"I don't really know much more son; your Mom was in a hurry to get there and I offered to give you a bit of dinner if she wasn't back! She just said that Pearl was taken poorly."

I hesitated by the kitchen door but Mrs Gould saw my hesitation and said, "Come on Josh, I don't bite, make yourself comfortable."

"Don't you think that I should make my way to the hospital, Mrs Gould? I can get there, I know the way!"

Mrs Gould was adamant, "No Josh! Don't be silly; I can't let you do that. Your Mom strictly asked that I should look after you, and that's what I'm doing, I feel responsible!"

"But, Mrs Gould!"

"No son, no ifs or buts; Pearl's in safe hands. I don't think that it can be anything too serious and your Mom shouldn't be too long!"

Reluctantly I sat down at her kitchen table but she reminded me to take off my school jacket and put my bag down. I hadn't even thought of that, so I did, and then I sat back down. I immediately started to tell her, "I'm concerned about Pearl and so is Mom; she hasn't been too well lately."

"Has she not, Josh? I've noticed that she's lost some

weight but I didn't think that she was poorly!"

Mrs Gould had done a lovely Irish stew, but I couldn't really do it justice; I ate about half of it and she asked if it wasn't to my taste, but I told her that it was grand but I'd lost my appetite. She asked me to go through into her living room, and she followed, and patted the back-rest of the armchair in front of the television, prompting me to sit down. I just did as I was asked; Mrs Gould is a formidable character! She went to fetch me some tea and I sat there thinking that, 'if she was right, and Pearl was really not too bad, at least we would know soon, and if I were to dash off to try to meet them, well, I could easily miss them and make matters worse.' So I decided that it was best to stay put. As it happened, I had a couple of cups of tea with Mrs Gould and a good chat about the old times with Dad and Mom, before Mrs Gould spotted an ambulance pulling up at our front gate. I looked at Mrs Gould's clock; it had just gone past six o'clock.

I watched through her bay window for a few moments and saw the driver open the rear doors and out stepped Mom; the driver then helped Pearl down and she looked okay. So I quickly grabbed my coat and bag and thanked Mrs Gould for her hospitality, before dashing to the door. I was down greeting Pearl when I heard Mrs Gould shouting to Mom, enquiring about Pearl's health, and Mom thanked her. She stood on the step and gave us a little wave; Pearl took a little red blanket from her shoulders and handed it to the driver. We thanked him before shutting the door behind us. Once inside I asked, "What happened, Mom?"

Mom helped Pearl into the comfy chair and put the fire on before answering, "She's just not been too well at work, Josh!"

Mom gave me a bit of a sign and headed towards the kitchen, saying, "I'll get you a hot drink, Pearl."

I followed behind her and once inside the kitchen, she softly said, "I didn't want to say much in front of her, Josh."

"Well, what do you mean, 'not too well'? What happened?"

"Sshhh! Josh, the floor supervisor at Woolworths said that, they'd found Pearl unconscious in the stockroom, but she also told me that Pearl has fainted about seven or eight times in the last three months and she assumed that I knew all about it. She'd told them that she was seeing a doctor!"

"But she isn't, Mom!"

"No! I knew that but she didn't!"

"So what did the hospital say?"

"They're concerned about Pearl's weight, her blood pressure and blood-sugar level. They told me that she's just a little heavier than four stone! Josh, I don't know what we're going to do with her. I couldn't believe it Josh, *four stone*!"

I went back in to Pearl and I knelt at her side; her eyes were dark and she looked tired and pale. I suppose I was both emotional and angry but I held her hand and spoke softly to her.

"This has got to stop Pearl. Do you hear me! It has to stop! If you keep on this way you know what will happen, don't you?"

Pearl had no fight in her and she simply replied, "I know Josh!"

Mom brought Pearl a hot chocolate drink through and was just securing it safely in her hands when I heard the back door open and close. Jack came peering through into the living room.

"Where's my dinner?" he asked.

He was as polite as ever and those were the first words he spoke.

"What's she doing sat in my chair?" were the second!

Mom caught hold of his arm and led him away; I heard him mumbling, "What yer doing woman?"

I sat with Pearl as she sipped at her chocolate; it was warm in front of the fire and I watched as a tiny bit of colour came back into her cheeks. I had confused thoughts; I was mad at the way Jack had thoughtlessly spoken, I was mad because of the way Pearl had chosen to react to what was happening in her life and strangely enough I felt she was a little bit selfish, giving up in the way that she was. This meant that I would be the only one left to fight against things! Suddenly, I also felt ashamed about being so unthoughtful about Pearl's present condition. So, trying to express my concern, I asked, "Why didn't you tell us that you had been fainting at work?"

Pearl took the mug away from her lips and said, "I didn't want to worry anyone! There's enough stress and worry in this house!"

"Oh Pearl, can't you see, it doesn't have to be like this, you don't have to make yourself ill!"

I paused for just a moment and then said, "Can't you see that I need you?"

Pearl spent a week at home; she lay in bed most of the time and whenever she got up she always complained of giddiness until she had settled into a chair for a while. I began bringing her a block of chocolate home every school day from the shop. She always thanked me but I never actually saw her eating it; she would always open it immediately and break off the first row to hand to me, but then she'd re-wrap it. I constantly asked if she wanted things to eat or drink, but Mom suggested that I should be more careful, because the hospital had given her some leaflets that said it was unhelpful to push food onto someone with this condition. I just didn't know what to do for the best! When Saturday arrived, Pearl seemed a little better and told Mom that she wanted to go with her shopping. I was concerned and asked Mom if she thought it was a good idea. Anyway, Pearl was adamant that she wanted to go. I grew anxious waiting but eventually they arrived back safely. Pearl eventually went back to work on Monday and I thought that things might be looking brighter! We walked together as normal and she chatted away happily but as she left me I asked her to take care.

For the next three weeks she seemed to be coping quite well and I knew that she was making a real effort. When we were at home, and Pearl was out of earshot, I asked Mom regularly how she thought that Pearl was doing. Mom always agreed that she too thought that things were looking brighter. I asked about her weight but Mom said that she hadn't asked. This I couldn't understand, surely it was extremely important to check that she was gaining weight? When I tackled Mom about it she said that the doctor had told her that she must be very careful not to keep pressurising Pearl!

It was the last half-term holiday before I finished completely at the school; that meant just another six weeks before a week's holiday and then I would be starting work at Uncle Fred's warehouse. I was a lot more excited about the money that I would start to have than the prospect. It would be good to have money of my own and perhaps then I might be able to help Pearl and Mom even more! I didn't really know Uncle Fred that well; he was Dad's brother and we'd seen more of him when Dad was alive, but since Dad had gone it had only been on the odd occasion. I knew that I was to work in a hardware warehouse and that I'd be handling boxes of nails, screws and stuff like that! But that was all I did know! I suppose I was too engrossed with the thought of the future and the fact that Mr Hullstone had taken this week off, and we'd been off out each day enjoying ourselves. We'd been swimming, and playing football in the park and, on the Wednesday morning, we'd even been to the Zoo; a place I hadn't been for a long, long time. I had begun to tell Pearl about the lions and polar bears, that I had seen, as soon as she had walked through the door. I remember how my enthusiasm at my own pleasure began to wane when suddenly it occurred to me how peaky Pearl looked again. She did have a laugh with me about some of the things that had happened that day and it appeared to brighten her a little. Looking back; I think it must have been the first time during that week, that I had paid enough attention to Pearl's looks, and it shocked me to see how loosely her little white blouse hung on her. She was so frail and I couldn't help but notice how yellowish her eyes were.

That night Pearl went up to bed at about 8.30-ish, that wasn't too unusual because she regularly went to bed early and Mom always thought that it was a good idea. She always popped in to see if Pearl had settled down okay when she was on her way to bed and, these days, Mom was usually in for 10.30pm. As long as I was never left alone with Shipley I would go to suit myself and there was loads of stuff in my room to keep me entertained if I wasn't too sleepy. That night as Mom was leaving Pearl's bedroom I met her on the landing and I asked if Pearl was okay. Mom said, "Yes, well she thought she was, why?" I just told her that, when I had been chatting to her earlier, I had noticed that her eyes looked very yellow. I asked if she had noticed them and she said that she hadn't! Then I asked if she knew whether or not Pearl had been regaining some of her lost weight, but Mom said that she wasn't really sure. It was then that I mentioned the way that Pearl's blouse seemed to hang so loosely on her. Mom seemed so nonchalant about it that I got a little upset because I was concerned, and Mom didn't appear to be. I think that she realised this straight away and she reassured me that she was keeping a close eye on her; she put her hand to my cheek and kissed me on the forehead.

That, for Mom, was a little bit unusual these days; I just said, "Goodnight" and went to bed.

I was up the next morning at about eight o'clock; it was Thursday the 29th of June, I was certain of that because I always changed my little perpetual calendar before I went downstairs. Mom was busy doing the breakfast and Jack had already gone off to work. Mom asked, "Have you heard anything of Pearl yet, Josh?"

I just replied, "No, why, haven't you?"

"No! She was still sound asleep when I looked in, and I didn't like to wake her!"

"She generally doesn't need any waking; she's usually messing about early, getting organised for work, she is in today isn't she?"

"Well she didn't mention anything else to me; she'll be late. Will you take her this tea up and tell her to get a move on!"

I carried Pearl's mug of tea carefully up the stairs and I rapped with my knuckles upon the door before pushing it open. Pearl's curtains were still closed; I noticed a strong smell of lavender in her room. She looked that peaceful as I stood by her bedside that I was concerned that I needed to disturb her. I touched her gently on her shoulder and placed the mug of tea upon her cabinet. She didn't awake and I noticed that she had the faintest of smiles upon her face. I went across the room and opened the curtains, expecting that the light would rouse her but as I stood there in the window she still lay silently. I went back to her and I stood and looked upon her pale face. Then I fell to my knees, screaming, and I screamed again and again until Mom came to my side, but Pearl had gone!

CHAPTER TWELVE

The Funeral

I only returned to school for three of those last remaining six weeks. I had no interest in school and I certainly had no interest in my future! There had to be an inquest into Pearl's sudden death and that took far too long. The whole of that period to me was just a heartbreaking blur! Once I was back at school Liam was a rock for me and he was there whenever I needed him. Even before that, he and his parents had spent longer at our home, comforting Mom and me, than they had done in many years. I believe now that it was only Mrs Hullstone that kept Mom sane throughout that period! I know that I did everything I could for Mom; but she was the one not only facing her sad loss, but also having to answer all the questions from the authorities. Pearl, we discovered, was just a little over three and a half stone at her death and I don't think that either of us had realised this! Jack was around but he was his normal self; he maintained throughout his ability to be callous and insensitive! He still turned up drunk on many occasions prior to the funeral, and he always expected his meals ready and waiting! I avoided his presence; we did not exchange conversation and I saw Jack as the overwhelming factor that our lives had been brought to this point.

At the funeral I was aware of just how many of Pearl's old school pals and work colleagues had turned up. It was heart-warming to see that so many people had really cared for her. Trevor was there too; he actually threw his arms around me and held me, with tears in his eyes! I was very upset that he was whisked away from us as soon as the funeral service was over. A lot of people came and spoke to us to say some really lovely and comforting things to Mom about Pearl and myself following the burial, where I was constantly at Mom's side. Jack kept a welcomed distance and appeared totally out of his comfort zone. Fortunately he said very little then but he failed to maintain this when we returned back to our home, where he truly revealed his character. I suppose some may say, on reflection, that I was provocative, but I simply spoke my mind. He had quickly opened up the whisky bottle on our arrival and started to become louder and more expressive; overbearing to say the least. He came over to me and said, "It was a good send-off lad, she was laid to rest decently!"

To which I immediately replied, "It's a pity it wasn't you!"

Jack caught hold of me by the wrist, dropping his glass to the carpet, and screamed, "What did you say?"

I looked across and saw that Mr Hullstone was watching us carefully, so bravely I replied, "You should have been in that box; you'd have done us all a favour!"

Without warning Jack struck me viciously with the back of his hand across my face and eye! His ring finger caught me in the eyelid and I reeled backwards from the blow! Liam, who was standing alongside me and had heard all of the conversation, instinctively caught hold of Jack's arm but he was thrown to one side. Mr Hullstone then wrestled Jack to the floor, and then out into the garden, where they continued to exchange punches! Throughout this, Mom and Mrs Hullstone were screaming for them to stop. When they were finally dragged apart the Hullstones left immediately and I overheard Mrs Hullstone's last words to Mom, that, "They would not return to the house again whilst Jack was under our roof!"

The morning after the funeral I looked at my face in the medicine cabinet; my eye was bloodshot and swollen and my eyelid was cut and looked gross! I was up late because I had no intention of going to school and I knew that Jack had already left the house because I had heard the slamming of doors! When I got downstairs Mom immediately wanted to look at my eye and fuss around me; she was very concerned at how bad it looked. She bathed it and she tutted and groaned; she put something on it that stung and made me wince, and she told me that I was a fool to taunt Jack! Then suddenly I realised that Mom had a split lip; it seemed swollen too.

"What happened to your lip?"

"Oh, it's nothing Josh, but you need that looking at!"

Mom touched at my cheek and I flinched from the pain and pulled back.

"Mom, did he do that to you?"

"Yes Josh, but let's leave it now, it all got out of hand and you should know what he's like. He's sorry this morning and he's told me that you were riling him!"

"Oh, so that's alright is it? To punch everyone around him because he doesn't like to hear the truth? I told him that it should have been him buried; that he should have been in that coffin, not our Pearl!"

I was angry and I cried; Mom put her arms around me and she cried too and she said quietly as she held me,

"That wasn't nice was it Josh? It shouldn't have happened to anyone!"

I immediately pulled away from her and said, "You see that it's all him, don't you, Mom?"

"What's all him?"

"Everything, he's the cause of it all, Mom! Don't you see?"

It was Friday the next day and I'd told Mom the

previous day that if the Hullstones did not contact us, then I would go around there. Mr Hullstone would be at work, I knew, but when I arrived Mrs Hullstone immediately showed me that there was no animosity between us by giving me a huge hug. Mom hadn't wanted me to go because she believed that things needed to be left alone for a while in order to cool down but I hadn't agreed with her; I believed that things needed sorting out. I knew now that I had been right. Mrs Hullstone started to make a huge fuss about my face, she got something from a bottle and dabbed it on to it. I told her that Mom had ended up with a split lip too but I didn't see it happen. Liam was at school but he came home before I left and he seemed very pleased to see me there. He begged me to go back into school on the following Monday and I told him that I had already decided to do that anyway. I left before Mr Hullstone returned from work because I wanted to be back at home for Mom just in case Shipley started again.

It was only when I came to put on my school blazer, on that Monday morning, that it suddenly struck me! I accepted that it wouldn't be for the first time, because there had been the odd occasion previously, but it was the realisation that I would be walking to school on my own! It didn't suddenly make me think of Pearl, because Pearl had never been out of my mind since 'that morning'. No, I think that it was the realisation of the practical loss. I just couldn't say anything to Mom; I didn't want to hurt her, so I just grabbed my bag and left for school. It was a very lonely walk and I was exceptionally glad to see the school gates and the sight of Liam appearing in the other direction. We had just about ten minutes before registration and Liam asked if I was okay. I told him how I'd felt and Liam told me that he understood and he knew how hard it must be, and he added, "It's hard for me too, you know?"

We were not together for the first two sets but I must say that everyone else who took the time to speak to me was extremely sympathetic, especially the girls who had known Pearl. It was very emotional to have to keep going over the same thing but they all meant well. I found it almost impossible to concentrate on my work; the English teacher was talking grammatical terms and my mind kept on drifting away. I found that my eyes kept focussing upon the empty sports field; it seemed so quiet. It was the loneliness and the emptiness that hit me the hardest. I kept telling myself that there were only three weeks left and that I would soon be leaving all of this behind me but there were occasions when the tears welled within my eyes. When I finished in three weeks, I knew too that I would be having another lonely week at home before starting out on my new working life. Uncle Fred had been at the funeral and he had tried to muster a bit of enthusiasm from me about my future, but I was in the wrong state of mind. Now sitting there, feeling lost, I still felt much the same; to me all the future seemed to be was one big black hole!

At lunchtime I sat with Liam, Jimmy Rogers and some other lads at their table; they were a bunch of lads just laughing and joking! They did their best to include me in everything they said and did, and most of them knew that I was normally up for a good laugh. Liam must have seen that I was attempting to put a brave face on things and he asked me, as we were leaving the dining hall, if I could meet them at the park later that day. I asked what they were going to do and he said that they were just generally going to mess about a bit by the park pool.

"What do you mean by, 'mess about'?" I asked.

Liam replied, "Jimmy knows where the key is kept to the lock on the warden's boat, so we generally take it across to the island and have some fun."

"What kind of fun; and how do you mean, 'he knows where the key is kept'?"

Liam explained, "When the boats are finished with, at the end of the day on the park pool, the 'parky' takes them across to the island and ropes them together but he has to bring one back, doesn't he? So he brings one back to the quay and he chains that one up. Well, there are seven big boulders along that quayside and the one night Jimmy saw the parky place the key under the middle boulder before he left."

I asked, "So you pinch the key?"

"No we don't 'pinch it', we just borrow it and take the boat across to the island, we always put it back!"

"Ain't that dangerous?"

"Well, yes, I suppose it could be but we just have a bit of fun, as I said, it don't cause any harm, does it?"

I asked, "What would your Dad say?"

"Dad? Bloody hell mate, I wished I hadn't have asked you now!"

I must have sounded like my Mom when I replied, "Don't be silly, I'm just concerned."

I know he must have just been trying to help me, seeing the way I was, and I realised that, when Liam sharply replied, "Well don't be, we don't do anyone any harm, do we?"

So I replied quietly, "No, I suppose you don't."

For a moment there was silence and then I enquired, "What 'fun'? You said that you had fun on the island."

"We just mess about; we had a right laugh the last time we did it. You know there are twenty four boats tied up and they're all side by side; we were seeing who could run the quickest across them. Well that's really difficult and it's awesome when they start bobbing up and down! Are you going to come then?"

I hesitated before replying, "I don't know, I'll see, what time anyway?"

"About six-ish, okay?"

"Yeah!" Liam then dashed away because we were late for our afternoon lessons.

But I didn't go that night. It wasn't because I didn't intend to, in fact I started out from home at about half-five-ish and I was probably within about ten minutes of reaching the park when I saw that Jack's car was parked again. I think it was in exactly the same spot where Mr Hullstone and I had seen it before. I wandered slowly past it, on the other side of the road. I could see that Jack was in there again, busy cheating on Mom! I was able to see clearly in the car from a position where I sat down on the embankment across the other side of the road. Although, I don't think that Jack would have noticed me if I had stood right in front of the car! He was a worthless git! I hated him! Mom did not deserve to be treated like this and I had this sudden rash thought of running back home and bringing Mom to the car so that she could see for herself! Instead I sat there thinking, 'what could make an adult accept this sort of situation'? Mom had said before that she believed me, so why did she let it go on? I just sat there until I watched Jack straightening up that slick black hair before driving away. I started away immediately to walk back home; I wanted to be there when he returned and I knew that he had to drop his floozy off. I wanted to hear him as he told his lies, and see the look upon that smug face as he deceived her once more. As it happened, he never even needed to lie because I heard Mom talking to him from the moment he walked in and whilst he ate his dinner in the kitchen; she never once remarked or enquired about where he had been, perhaps she just accepted it! I was going to tell her later but I thought, 'why should I be the one who continues to hurt her, she'd rather close her eyes to it and that way there was no hurt!'

The next day at school, Liam asked why I hadn't gone to the park and I told him about what I had seen. Liam thought that I should take greater care because I knew what Jack was like and that he may easily have caught me spying on him. He told me that he was sorry, but then suddenly he switched to telling me what a great laugh they'd all had again. Well they'd had a laugh up until Robbie Lloyd apparently had gone in up to his waist! I asked how that had happened and Liam told me that they were running on the boats again, and he and some of the others were positioned along the line of boats; they all took a turn in running the boats and when Robbie took his, well, some of the lads were bobbing the boats a bit high. Robbie got about three parts of the way and then Jake had lifted his too high, causing Robbie to miss his footing! Robbie slipped off the edge of the boat but managed to hang on to the side, halfway in the water! Jake dragged him out and they had to light a fire on the island to help dry him out before they could all go home and it had made them late. I asked if he had had to tell his Mom and Dad then, but he replied, "You must be joking!" He said that I should go next time but I was still concerned especially after hearing about Robbie. I told him that I was worried that someone might get hurt, but Liam seemed to think that, because quite a few of them went, there was safety in numbers. They watched out for one another. I suppose that I must have come over as a bit of a 'wuss' but the idea of him taking these risks bothered me.

Before I knew it, the end of the term had arrived and we were sat in the leavers' assembly. I think that the majority of the lads were looking forward to starting their jobs; Liam was particularly enthusiastic about his apprenticeship, although he'd realised that the starting pay would not be that good. Some of the lads who were starting jobs in factories had rubbed it in with Liam; jibing about how much they were going to earn. I had no enthusiasm whatsoever; I was looking forward to my week off and that was all. I found the final day at school to be very emotional and I was glad when it all came to an end. We didn't do any real school stuff; I think that's what made it drag on. We watched a film, played a bit of sport and ended up signing each other's shirts and ties. Liam and I hung about a bit outside the school along with a few other mates and he asked me to go over to his house during the week; he promised that he would phone during the weekend to make arrangements. I knew that his Dad had not got the week off, so we wouldn't be going out anywhere with him. Liam had already told me that he and Jimmy were going fishing on the Wednesday. I expected that Uncle Fred would phone me or Mom sometime during the week but he never did. All that I knew was that I was supposed to be at the warehouse for 8.00am on the morning that I was starting. Mom had bought me some overalls and a workbag with a flask in it. So like it or hate it, my week off was about to commence and then, after that, work!

It was a hard job. I very rarely saw anything of Uncle Fred and I saw a lot less of my home and Liam. All I seemed to do was haul heavy boxes about; square, dusty boxes. They were full of nails, screws, springs, pins or levers of varying descriptions. I started off by doing nine hours a day but soon I was also doing overtime and I never failed to return home exhausted. I had to climb up amongst racks of shelving and locate and bring down whatever I was given requisitions for, then I would gather them together before loading them onto various vans for delivery. In the first few weeks I seemed to ache in every bone of my body.

Soon, I had muscles appearing where I had never seen muscles before. I had money too – more money than I had ever seen in my life – and that meant that every time I did meet up with Liam, I was able to treat him. I knew that he had a good job as an apprentice and he seemed to be really enjoying every moment of it. He had to do one day and night a week at the local Technical College but he said that his money was rubbish and would be for some time to come yet. I used to meet him in the local café and sometimes we would go into town on the Saturday afternoons. One benefit at home was that, because of my new income, Mom seemed to be becoming more independent of Jack. She started back at the Co-Op too, not long after I had started the job; she only did the few odd afternoons but that meant that she was also earning herself. She had my keep coming in and some money of her own and I noticed that she was less of a rubbing rag for Jack; she started answering back more often.

If it were at all possible then Jack was even more of a grump than ever. He no longer had Pearl to abuse so he turned more and more towards me; anything he mislaid I was to blame for. To him, I was always in the way and he was forever saying that I was an 'idle git'! He never raised a finger to help Mom about the house but I did. After I'd been at the warehouse for twelve months Jack scared me less and less. His insults and his pettiness bounced off me. I'd put on weight and was well-built; with the beer gut that he now had, I saw him as no match for me. I began believing that, if I needed to, I could take him at any time and would not hesitate. Fortunately for me, I saw less of him now than I had ever done. I was a little surprised that he and Mom hadn't collided over her work because sometimes she didn't get in until after 7.00pm; that meant that he had to wait for his dinner but I suppose that it also meant that he could take longer about getting home too. He was probably getting less hassle and more satisfaction. The latest I worked until was 6.00pm, that meant I could have a bath and get changed before Mom was home, and have the meal ready, then I would settle down in front of the television with my dinner. They sat in the kitchen to eat and that too suited me. I never ate with him; if there was something he really wanted to see on the television then I'd take my food upstairs and I just loved the occasions when he wasn't about at all and Mom and I could eat together.

I think Jack became jealous of my new-found independence but mainly he was more annoyed at my continual refusal to be his lackey; running his errands and generally being at his beck and call. I no longer desired or required two shillings or five shillings! I always seemed to have more money in my pocket than he did. His was either wasted on booze or spent on his floozies. Yes, there still were 'floozies'; I knew it and so did Mom! Jack and I still had loads of disagreements and it was simply for Mom's sake only that, for the moment, I took it no further. Mom seemed to prefer to be left in the dark; she didn't want to know about what he was doing as long as he kept it well away from her ears and out of our sight!

During the next summer holiday period I had the longest of my breaks from the job; our warehouse had a two week summer lay-off because most of our customers were off too. Liam and I were lucky that my second week off coincided with a week of his holiday. We were able to do loads of stuff together, and Mr Hullstone had the Wednesday off, so he took Liam and his Mom and me to Bridgnorth for the day. We had a great day; the sun shone, we had a meal out in a restaurant and I just wished that Mom could have been there too enjoying herself. There was one thing I now knew that I hated most about working; the lack of holidays! They were few and far between and I had to take them to suit the warehouse, not myself. I did not want to go back to work; as the end of the week grew near, I became more and more aware of this. Worse still I knew that Liam would still be off and that he and Jimmy would be off doing stuff together. Liam had told me that they had things planned but I could do nothing about it! I suppose there was some jealousy on my part but mainly I missed the long summer holidays of school time. One thing that would never have entered my mind, though, was that the week that we had just spent together would forever remain one of the most special weeks of my life.

***

Two weeks later I sat next to Jimmy and he told me all about their week together; it seemed as hard for him as it was for me, but I needed to know, and gradually I encouraged him to tell me everything. Like everyone else, I had heard the sketchy details but Jimmy was actually there with Liam and I wanted to know everything; just how and why it had happened. I knew that it would hurt me and now I could see and appreciate just how much it hurt Jimmy too. I knew that I just wouldn't be able to live my life without knowing; so I asked him, "Please tell me about it?"

He replied, "It's difficult, you know Josh. I still find it very hard, it hurts me so much! I've had to go through it over and over again; it's torture!"

I put my hand to his shoulder; he had lowered his head and he lifted it slowly.

"I know how hard it must be Jimmy, but I need to know, I couldn't live my life through without ever knowing!"

I could see that he had tears in his eyes and I felt exactly the same.

"We went out on the Monday, Tuesday and the Wednesday and we had some laughs. We'd been fishing twice and we went to the cinema on Wednesday when it was raining. Oh, and we also went to the baths on Monday and some of the other lads came with us."

He hesitated once more and I knew that he was avoiding getting to the Thursday, "On the Wednesday when we left the cinema I suggested that, if it was decent weather the following day, then we should go to the park. He was keen, and by 10 o'clock on the Thursday the sun was shining, so I gave him a call and arranged to meet him."

Jimmy stopped again in order to compose himself and then went on, "We met by the park gates and walked down passed the fountain; although it was nice we only saw two other people; Liam had a tennis ball in his pocket and when he pulled it out we had a bit of a kick-about, just for about ten minutes or so, then we ended up rolling down the bank towards the pool. There was no one about and I didn't know what he was intending to do, but when he got up he went over and got the key to unlock the boats. We took the boat over, same as we'd done the times before, and we began messing about on the boats. Liam used to stand up and rock the boat from side to side; this time I thought we were going in so I jumped onto another boat. Liam just laughed at me and then he attempted to jump after me into my boat but one of the oars caught between his legs and the boat."

Jimmy hesitated again before going on, "The boat he was in sort of pushed backwards in the water, and he fell towards me striking his head on the side of my boat! He went under. It all happened so quickly. I shouted but I couldn't see him so I pushed my hand downwards as far into the water as I could. I couldn't feel a thing, but then suddenly he shot upwards at the end of the boat, completely out of my reach, but he made no sound. I scrambled to get over to him and my boat tipped and I ended up in the water, but I never saw Liam again. I waited and waited, all the time screaming as loud as I could; no one came, so then I jumped from the water and ran to the park gates. There was a bloke passing by and I begged him for help and he said he'd phone someone. It must have been about fifteen minutes before an ambulance arrived, and the parky."

"It took them about ten minutes to find him and they dragged him from the water with a long barge pole! I'm sorry mate, but there was nothing anyone could do!"

Jimmy struggled to hold back the tears and I felt sorry for him – sorry that I'd put him through it all again – but I needed to know.

CHAPTER THIRTEEN

The Final Steps

It was Saturday morning; a miserable day about three months after Liam's death. I was just sitting in the 'Rio'; the same café that Liam and I had used regularly. I was the only customer in there and Charlie, the owner, was standing wiping cups at the counter. He'd been attempting to make a little small talk but I wasn't too responsive. The window was steamed up and I used my knuckles to wipe the mist to one side. I was about half-way down a mug of hot chocolate, and lost in my thoughts. Charlie dropped a mug and it smashed to the ground causing me to look up, startled. Charlie's head rose from below the counter and there was a clanging as the shards of broken mug hit the steel bin. Charlie mumbled a few expletives and then appeared, for some unknown reason, to be pointing in my direction. I then realised that he was pointing beyond me and through the window. I turned, only to be startled again with the sight of a nose flattened hard against the window where I had just rubbed clear. It pulled away to reveal Jimmy Rogers! The door swung open and the bell on the door tinkled.

"Alright, Josh, I thought it was you!"

Jimmy pushed the door shut behind him and crossed to the counter.

"Can I get you something, Josh?"

I stalled a moment, said, "No," and then said, "Oh, okay then, I'll have another hot chocolate please."

I'd never seen Jimmy in the café before but it was

pretty obvious that he and Charlie knew one another. They chatted about the rain and Charlie enquired about Jimmy's Dad's health.

He pushed my chocolate across the table towards me as he sat down opposite. He'd got himself a chocolate too.

"You okay, mate?" he asked.

"Yes thanks how about you?"

"Not too bad! I didn't know that you came in here."

"Yeah, I used to come in here a lot with Liam."

Surprisingly he replied, "Yeah, so did I!"

I hadn't seen Jimmy since we'd had that 'last' conversation together. He was never someone whom I bumped into a lot, and somehow his relationship with Liam made it a little bit more difficult to be in his company. I didn't know why, it was inexplicable, but it just felt awkward.

"What you up to?" he enquired.

"Oh, nothing, I just got out of the house, I don't like spending too much time there when he's about!"

I didn't know if Jimmy knew anything of my relationship with Shipley but he said, "That bloke's an idiot; I don't like him. Liam used to tell me about the way he treated you, and my Dad said, he wouldn't trust the bloke as far as he could throw him!"

I felt myself suddenly warming towards Jimmy and his Dad, whom I'd never actually met. There was still a side of me that wanted to punch Jimmy straight in the mouth for his part in Liam's death but the other side argued that Jimmy was no more responsible than I was! He suddenly asked how my job was going and I replied, "Okay mate, if you can call work that; it's hard labour but the money's good. How about you, how you getting on?"

"Same here, I don't think that you do it for the fun, do yer?"

"No mate, I don't suppose yer do!"

He took a long drink from his hot chocolate and lowered the mug to reveal a moustache of froth around his lips; I grinned and he suddenly realised why and brushed it to one side. Then he asked, "What yer doing later?"

"Later when?"

"Well this afternoon?"

"I dunno, why?"

"I was thinking of going to see that 'Ben Hur' film at the Clifton but I hate sitting in the flicks on me own!"

I enquired, "'Ben Hur', what's that about?"

He looked surprised, "Blimey mate, everyone's on about it!"

"Oh, I don't know what is it then?"

"Well it's Roman or Greek or something; I think John Wayne's in it!"

Charlie laughed; he was obviously listening in to our conversation and he said, "It ain't John Wayne it's Charlton Heston; I saw it on Wednesday night, it's brilliant! Especially the chariot race!"

We both looked across at him a little surprised, and then looked back at each other. Jimmy whispered, "Nosey git!" And we both laughed.

I hadn't thought about going to the pictures in a long time – not since I'd last been with Liam – and I too was like Jimmy and hated sitting in a cinema on my own. For some unknown reason I said yes, and we asked Charlie if he had a paper and he threw one to us. Jimmy checked the cinema times and we agreed to meet at 2.30pm, that afternoon.

Ben Hur was a great film, especially the chariot race (so the nosey git had been right!) but it lasted a hell of a while and I hadn't realised just how long. Darkness was just beginning to fall as we walked from the cinema and just around the corner Jimmy patted my arm and said, "ain't that yer Dad?" I looked up and saw Shipley heading towards us and he wasn't on his own. There clinging to his arm, was the same blonde bimbo as I'd seen him with before! Of course he was much too busy to notice me, and I quickly pulled Jimmy to one side to avoid crossing paths with him.

"What's the matter?" he asked.

"Well firstly, he's not me bloody Dad and secondly he's with his bit on the side again."

Jimmy saw how angry I was and he offered his apologies, "I'm sorry mate."

"I hate him, I hate his guts and wish me Mom had never clapped eyes on him!"

There they were all lovey-dovey and I knew that me Mom was probably back at home, doing his tea, and thinking he was doing overtime.

"How long's he been seeing her then?" Jimmy asked.

"A while mate, but he'll get his eventually!"

"How d'yer mean?"

"I don't know yet, but he will!"

When I got back home I told Mom that I'd seen him with her again but she just said she didn't want to know. What could I do to make her see sense? After a brief moment of quietness, she asked, "How was the film?"

I told her that it had been good and that she should go and see it. Then there was another short lull in the conversation and I looked at her searchingly and suddenly I felt so sorry for her. She wasn't the Mother that I had known as I was growing up as a small child. I saw the lines upon her face; the darkness around her eyes, and the grey that was appearing all over her hair. My mind was in torment; I couldn't take much more of this! But I had no idea just how to put things right. Then I saw the tiniest of tears roll down her cheek and she swiftly reacted by brushing it to one side. I immediately went to her and embraced her; I loved her so much and I was aware that both of our hearts were breaking.

Three hours later the phone rang and it was Shipley. The first words that I heard from Mom were that his tea was still in the oven, and when would he be home? I heard nothing for the next few minutes and then I heard Mom saying, "It's alright, don't worry, I understand. I'll see you as soon as you can get back then. I hope that she'll be okay, bye." She came back into the kitchen to where we had both been sitting together, since her tears, reminiscing about the past and therefore avoiding the present.

I asked, "What's up, Mom?"

"It was Jack, he said that his sister in Scotland had been taken ill and he's had to go up there straight from work!"

"I didn't know that he had a sister in Scotland?"

"He's got two sisters; they were both at the wedding, can't you remember them?"

"No!" I replied.

"When will he be home then?" I enquired (wishing that he'd stay away forever).

"He doesn't really know!"

"Has he got time off work?"

"Not that I know of, but I suppose if it's an emergency then he has to have it!"

With slight hesitation, I asked, "Do you believe him, Mom?"

And she honestly replied, "I just don't know what to believe any longer, Josh! And I don't really think that it makes any difference!"

I, for one, did not, and recognised Shipley for the liar that he was!

It was four days before we saw him again and I had been more than grateful for the respite!

In those four days Mom did not receive a single

telephone call, and she herself, had no number to contact. On the day he arrived home we were both sat watching television, in the living room. We saw Jack walk across the front of the house, arm in arm with the same blonde that Jimmy and I had seen him with that day after the film. Both Mom and I immediately spoke in unison, "Is that Jack?"

It was, and he walked back into our home with what I'd describe as, 'a reasonable suntan'!

It was most definitely the same blonde, there was no mistaking that, and I just could not believe, even knowing him for what he was, that Jack would have the audacity to try this on! He introduced her to Mom by saying, "You remember Margaret, don't you? My sister."

I could see that Mom looked at her with uncertainty, but she replied, "Of course I do, Jack!"

She stood up to greet her, and said hello to this woman, I remained firmly in my seat and when Mom suggested that I should say hello, I nodded my head with disdain.

"How are you now?" Mom asked.

The blonde glanced sideways at Jack, smiled and replied, "Not too bad!"

"Have you eaten, Jack? We've not long had ours, but I can do something for you and Margaret," Mom politely enquired.

I just could not believe that I was witness to this charade!

Jack replied, "We could do with a cup of tea, but otherwise we're okay. We have stopped for a meal on the way down."

He then offered Margaret a seat before following Mom into the kitchen. Margaret sat across from where I sat and she smiled and said hello. I nodded once more out of politeness but said nothing. I could now see that her blonde hair was in fact dyed! She was slim and was indeed very pretty but her clothes were too young for her age. I had no respect for her because she knew the position that she was in; she was not an innocent victim caught up in this nonsense. I could hear Jack and Mom talking in the kitchen, just briefly, and then Jack came back through and said, "Come on, Marg, I'll show you your room!"

I waited until I heard the stairs begin to creak and I went immediately through to Mom.

"What's going on?" I asked.

"Margaret needs to stop here for a while, only a few days, and I've told Jack that it will be okay."

I raised my voice, "Bloody hell, Mom! We don't want his floozy here!"

Mom shushed me abruptly and pushed the door shut.

"Please don't cause a scene, Josh!"

I looked at her in disbelief.

"Is it me, or is everything going mad around here?"

Mom shushed again.

"She'll only be here a few days!"

I snatched open the door and rushed into the hallway grabbing my coat before slamming the door as I left! I just could not get my head around this; how could Mom be so stupid and how had he got the nerve? Sister, my arse! Did Mom actually believe him? I couldn't possibly see how any sane person could! I decided, as I walked, that Mom had lost the will to fight!

I strode around one road after another, just seething and walking. There was no direction or purpose, just a burning desire to get away and escape that Mad-House! I eventually found myself outside the Rio and who should I find sat inside; Jimmy Rogers. I just had to speak to someone and Jimmy filled that role. Jimmy must have been fed up to the back teeth with me as I raved on and on endlessly, until eventually I ran out of wind. To be fair, Jimmy just sat there absorbing it all, listening and nodding sympathetically. For me, it was enough that I was given the outlet just to express how bitterly exasperated I was and to blow off steam! Jimmy patiently studied me as I stuttered to a halt, wondering if or not he should step in or was this another pause for breath? He bravely spoke,

"Why don't you come home with me?"

I replied, "I can't do that!"

"Why not? I'm sure that my Mom would be alright about it, I've told her about the way things are!"

Jimmy's offer was very tempting but I knew that, if I wanted to, I could have gone to the Hullstones, but I just could not do that.

"No; it's a very tempting offer Jimmy, but I can't leave me Mom in that position."

I would dearly have loved to have got away and escaped that life; the adult world where nothing any longer made sense to me. I knew that, deep down, I could not leave Mom with Jack, and who knew what idiocy might proceed?

***

When I got home from work the following day, I knew that Mom would still be working. It was Friday night, her late night at the Co-Op. Normally Jack would have still been out too; either at the pub, or doing 'overtime'. Tonight, as I discovered, it appeared that he was doing overtime at home. His car was outside and when I entered the house, I could hear the pair of them, upstairs, in Trev's room. I decided not to sneak about quietly but instead to behave as I normally would. Normally though I would have gone straight upstairs, to have a bath and remove the dust and grime of the warehouse. I had no intentions of going upstairs and walking into a geriatric clinch. So, I made enough noise for them to appreciate my presence. Jack eventually emerged, stumbling down the stairs in his vest and pants – not a pleasant sight! He ignored me and went through into the kitchen, where I could hear mugs clinking and the kettle being filled. I did not believe it when he shouted through, "Do you want a cuppa?"

I didn't answer and he repeated, "Do you want a cuppa?"

"NO!" I blasted.

He peered into the room and asked, "What's up with you?"

I replied, "I'm waiting to use the bloody bathroom!"

His retort was, "Well use, 'the bloody bathroom', there's no one in there!"

I dashed upstairs. All of the bedroom doors were shut so I tried the bathroom door; there was no one in there, so I slammed the door shut behind me and slid the bolt across. I ran the bath taps, pulled my underclothes from the airing cupboard and stripped off. I must have lain in that bath for an hour, until the water became unbearable and then I dressed, unbolted the door and went and hid myself in my own bedroom. I didn't hide in the true sense, but just because I did not want to be in their company, and I no longer knew how I might react.

When Mom came home I heard the door close behind her and so I immediately ran downstairs. Jack and the floozy were sitting in the living room, in front of the telly, all nice and cosy. I followed Mom into the kitchen, where she was already beginning to get stuff from the freezer in preparation for our meal. Neither Jack nor his crumpet had any intentions of helping out. I whispered to Mom about what was going on when I had returned from work and she said that she was fed up of hearing about it! She said that she was tired after work and just wanted to come home to a little peace for once and that she was sick of the whole thing. I could see that I was making things worse for her so I just lay off. I began helping Mom, I felt truly sorry for her because to me now, well, she just appeared a broken woman. She no longer had a passion for life; it was as if there was no way out, no response that she could make would improve her predicament. She'd given up and no longer tried to improve things; she'd just opted for a quiet life without all the hassle. I did ask her if she had any poison for the food, but she did not appreciate the black humour. In fact she insisted that I should behave myself and tread very carefully around Jack. She grabbed my wrist and whispered softly that I was all that she had in life now, the one thing that she could cling to.

Two weeks passed by and Mom said nothing to Jack, at least within my earshot but I began to pester him. If Mom didn't want that woman out, I did! I tried at first to be subtle (very difficult when the hate is immense)! Jack kept up the pretence that the blonde was his sister and, whilst Mom was about, he didn't flaunt their relationship. However, he was less pretentious on my behalf. In fact, he couldn't have cared less! He took us both for idiots and so I regularly enquired about how his sister's health was now. I asked if there was any support for her back in Scotland and regularly suggested that she might be better off there, in her home surroundings. I even suggested that he might move up there with her. His response was varied; sometimes he was as subtle as I was, but there were other occasions when such comments met with an anger and foul language!

I saw Jimmy Rogers on a few occasions during that couple of weeks and he asked for constant updates. I also visited the Hullstones and told them about the situation. Liam's Dad suggested that I should be patient, tread carefully and respect my Mother's wishes. Patience is a virtue; that's what my Dad taught me to believe and, as Mr Hullstone suggested, rashness now might only lead to nasty resolutions. My patience was running out! In the third week the first blows were struck! I caught the pair of them romping again, half naked, in the living room. Firstly I told Jack just what I thought of him and then I told her that she was a slut! Jack struck out at me and he half caught me with what was a glancing blow; I was agile enough to see it coming and I was fit. I swung only once at him but my contact was full on! He went out like a light! The blonde screamed her head off! She jumped up and down like a rag doll and screamed abuse at me before cradling Jack in her arms. I took the opportunity to look down upon my conquest and then walked away proudly. I had the biggest smile upon my face; there had been very little to smile about in the recent past, I felt immense, it had been too long in coming. I'd broken the chains and no longer would Jack have the upper-hand. Since my skirmishes at school, in those previous few years, I had not had a real confrontation with anyone, especially one that had led to punches being thrown. Jack would no longer torment Mom or me; I had broken that iron grip and there would be no return. I left the house slamming the door behind me, and I went straight to Jimmy's house. I told him what I had just done and it was not difficult in persuading him to join me for a pint; the first pint that I had ever bought in a pub! I replayed the situation several times for Jimmy's gratification; he was as chuffed as me. We sat there and gloated over my recollection of the events before I realised that Mom would be walking back into the house at any minute and I didn't know what welcome she might receive.

When I returned home, neither Jack nor Margaret were around but Mom sat alone in the kitchen. Immediately I saw her face all swollen up on one side and I realised that Jack had taken his revenge on her. I asked where he was; Mom said that he was in bed in Trev's room with 'her'. This was the first time that he had blatantly slept with the blonde in disrespect of Mom. I wanted to go up and drag them both from the bed, sling them from the house upon their arses, and throw their belongings through the bedroom window! Mom restrained me and she pleaded with me until I gave in. I told her that he had to go and that this was his final move! I asked about her face and she told me that there had been one almighty row when she had got home which resulted in Jack saying that, from now on, he would sleep with Margaret. Apparently Mom had tried to prevent him from going upstairs with her and this resulted in the backhand that she had received across her face! Knowing now that I had no fear of him, I told Mom that he would not torment us or destroy our lives any longer, but I respected Mom's wishes and left things as they were for that night because that was what she wanted. In the morning I would tell him in no uncertain words that both he and his crumpet should sling their hook! Mom finally agreed with me that this was what she wanted too; that she knew he had to go. At last, she had seen sense and no longer wanted him there. I did not leave the next morning until I had told him to be gone before I returned that night; I expected more and was ready for it but he just sat there and took it. I believed that I had made things clear!

All that day I couldn't wait for the time to come until I could get home to find our house back to how it used to be. I remember leaving work; I remember walking down the lane, and I remember turning the corner, but then the lights went out! Whatever hit me, I never saw it coming. It was dusk and there was no one around but suddenly I had been downed and I haven't been able to remember anything else whatsoever of that moment. I spent three days in hospital.

When Mom visited me, later that night, I remember only glimpses of her as I must have lapsed in and out of consciousness. It wasn't until the following day's visits, and talking with Mom, that I eventually gained any recollections of the events. I also learned that Jack had not gone; apparently both of them were still there and still sleeping together. Mom, however, believed that Margaret's departure was imminent. There had been discontent since the events of the last week had occurred, and the floozy apparently seemed to be making plans to leave. I could do nothing but lie there on my drips, with monitors constantly tracing my progress. Mom urged me to forget Jack and all of the hassle back home in order to get well. She assured me that he was having little, if anything, to do with her, and there had been no further confrontations. During the afternoon of the fourth day, I found out that I was going to be allowed to leave the hospital. They were content with my progress, as long as I remained sensible at home. I had twelve stitches to two wounds on the rear of my head, so when I phoned Mom she hired a taxi to come and collect me. I wondered why the Hullstones had not been, or indeed collected me from hospital, but it turned out that Mom hadn't told anyone about what had happened. So that also meant that Jimmy must have been unaware too. When we arrived home the house was empty; neither Jack nor the blonde were around. I prayed that we had seen the last of the pair of them. I had to go to bed straight away; I was still light-headed and had a bad headache. If Jack had have been there, I was in no position for a confrontation.

I spent another two days in bed at home; mainly because I kept feeling dizzy every time I tried to get up. Mom was doting on me; I suppose it was a chance to show once more that her Motherly nature was still active. Whilst I was in bed I never saw anything of Jack but I knew that he was still around, and Mom had told me that the blonde had gone on the morning of my return from hospital. Jack was still going out each morning to his job and Mom had been able to keep things going with hers too – always making sure that I was contented before she left home – so it was very quiet around the house. On the third day I made a real effort to get up; I sat at the edge of the bed until I felt reasonably sound and then I got myself into the bathroom where I soaked my face over and over in cold water, whist sitting on the edge of the bath. I don't know why but I then instinctively got to my feet and wandered into Mom's bedroom where I stood looking through the window onto the front lawn and the street. I noticed that Mrs Gould was in the garden doing a bit of weeding but she couldn't see me. I sat back on the edge of Mom's bed from where I could still see the street and people passing by. Mom had told me that Jack was still sleeping in Trev's room and in fact she'd told him that she did not want him back in hers. I looked around for any belongings of Jack's or of his previous presence, but I saw nothing. After a few minutes I got up and went to what had been his side of the bed, and glanced about; suddenly I noticed that the baseball bat was still in the alcove, leant against the wall next to the bed. I picked it up and to my amazement I could see what appeared to be stains on it, stains that I knew had definitely not been there before. I walked across to the light switch, switched it on and held the bat under the lamp; holding it closer to my eyes I could see a few hairs in the stain. They must have been stuck there as the blood congealed. I felt a little cold shiver as I realised that this was actually blood, I was sure that it was! I'd believed, from the moment that I had regained consciousness, that Jack had somehow been involved with what had happened to me. Now I knew it was Jack's doing. The trouble was, I knew that I was still not fit enough to confront him but I knew that I would do and I knew that he had to go, how, I didn't know but he had to!

Mom came home first; she was always there before Jack who had returned to his previous routine of 'overtime' and the booze. Mom was surprised to find me sitting in the kitchen. When she entered the hall I immediately heard her call upstairs as she had been doing the previous days before bringing me up a cuppa. She responded to my reply by wandering into the kitchen with a smile on her face.

"Are you sure that you're alright to be down here yet Josh?"

"I'm okay," I replied.

I'd just made my own mug of tea and got up to make one for Mom as she took off her coat and went into the hall to hang it up. She sat down by me and thanked me.

"It's nice to see you up and about again, but I hope it's not too soon!"

I reassured her that I didn't feel too bad.

"How long have you been down then?" she enquired.

"Only an hour or so."

She stroked my head softly and said, "That appears to be healing well."

"When have the stitches got to be taken out?"

"They haven't; remember that the nurse said that, they'd dissolve!"

"No! Did she?"

"Yes, apparently they do now; you just have to go back next Friday morning for a check-up. All that she said was that if you had bad headaches or any sickness then we could go back anytime. You're okay, aren't you love?"

"Yes, course I am, Mom. Don't you worry!"

Mom smiled and drank from her tea. A moment elapsed and I said, "I've been in your bedroom Mom."

She looked at me inquisitively and enquired, "What for,

were you looking for something?"

"No Mom, but I did find something!"

"What?"

"The baseball bat!"

"Oh! That old thing; is that still there?"

"Yes, and it's been used!"

"How'd you mean, 'used'?"

"There's blood and hair on it, Mom!"

Her face drained in shock.

"You're not serious are you, Josh?"

"It was Jack, Mom, didn't you suspect as much? Jack clobbered me from behind with the bat because of the threats I made to him; it was his style to hit me from behind, in the dark!"

Mom jumped up from her chair and marched off upstairs with me in pursuit. She went straight to the baseball bat and picked it up. I switched on the light to make it easier to see but I also suggested that she should take it closer to the window. She stood there rolling it around in her hands, examining it. After a few moments of deliberation, she spoke, "It could be red paint!"

"It's not red paint, it's blood! Remember when we looked at it before, when I first asked about it? Well, it wasn't there then, was it?"

I held the bottom half of the bat and turned it slowly into the light, "See there, tiny hairs stuck into it! Do they look the same colour as my hair; because I think they do?"

Mom pulled it away from my grip and examined it even closer; she picked at one of the tiny hairs with her finger nails. She managed to remove one and held it up between her fingers and against the light of the window glass. I could see it dawning upon her face and I knew that she believed me.

"He's got to go Mom! He'll stop at nothing! I'll leave it

another couple of days because I know that I'm not strong enough to deal with him at the moment, but he has to go!"

Mom returned the bat to the bedside where it had stood and I told her to say nothing about it; I didn't think that it was safe to confront him and I didn't want Mom to do so either. She reluctantly agreed, but I didn't know how long for!

"Where's all his stuff now, Mom?"

"He's taken most of his bits and pieces into Trev's room but he's still got clothes in the cupboard."

I asked, "Is that his leather case on the wardrobe?"

She said that it was.

So I reached it down.

"What you doing?" she asked.

"I'm going to take all his stuff out of this room and then perhaps he'll finally get the message!"

"Where you going to put it?"

"Oh, don't worry, I'm only going to put it in the other room but at least he'll know that he's not wanted, and if he doesn't get that message, then in a few days time we'll see!"

Mom grew concerned, "You'll only start him off Josh, please take care!"

I filled the case as Mom threw his things from the cupboards; there wasn't enough room in the suitcase, so Mom fetched a black plastic bin bag. I dragged them both through into Trev's room and dumped them at the foot of the bed. Mom shouted back from her room, "How about the bat, won't he think it's strange that we've left that?"

"Just leave it, Mom! It's best that he doesn't suspect that we've even noticed that; he'll just think that we've overlooked it!"

I went back through to her room and I noticed that the bat had gone, so I asked, "Didn't you hear me say to leave it?"

She replied, "Yes, but I'm scared that he might use it again, so I've hid the bloody thing!"

"Where you put it?"

She thought a moment and then said, "I think that it's best that only I know that, Josh!"

Mom then said, "Are you sure that it wouldn't be best to go to the police, Josh?"

I replied, "I just want him out of our lives Mom and I'm pretty sure now that you do too; how long do you think it would take the police to deal with it? And just think the way he'd behave in that time! Keep it safe, we might need the Police to see that if anything else should happen!"

When Jack returned late that night he had been drinking heavily. I considered, for a short time, whether this was a real opportunity to confront him but I was still feeling light-headed. He ignored me and I just sat there in the living room, watching the telly but keeping an eye open. He went straight through to the kitchen where Mom was doing him some tea. I could hear him stumbling about, chuntering on, but there was no real conversation between the pair of them. Until I heard him shout,

"What the bloody hell do you call this?"

Mom replied, "It's your dinner!"

Then I heard the plate smash and I immediately jumped up. I had to steady myself because of my swift movement. When I got into the kitchen Jack's plate was lying smashed against the far wall, and there was gravy and bits of food running down the wall. Jack had his back to me and he was struggling to reach his whisky bottle from the shelf. Mom started to cry and got up and went upstairs. For a brief moment I could see myself jumping upon Jack's back and bashing him against the tile floor, but instead I instinctively turned and followed Mom. When I got to her, she was lying face down upon her bed sobbing, so I comforted her. We stayed up there because of the way Jack was, but we said very little. If it had not been for my condition then that was the time and place that I knew that I too would have lost it! Mom was very frightened that when he came upstairs he would blow his top about his stuff. I just thought that he'd probably be too drunk to even notice it; anyway what was done was done! We listened to him down below; moaning, groaning and swearing, but he made no attempt to follow us.

At ten o'clock I suggested that Mom should get into bed and, when I left, she should put something against the door; I said I'd listen out for him. She was concerned for my safety and I told her that my door was more secure than hers and that I'd be ready for him! I didn't like leaving her but she reassured me that she would be fine; so I kissed her goodnight and left, listening to hear that she had secured the door behind me.

I lay in bed upon my back, just listening, and I knew that in this position I generally couldn't sleep anyway. It gradually went quiet down below and I was beginning to think that he'd probably collapsed upon the sofa and nodded off. I watched the clock tick round till 12.15am. I was so tired but I forced myself to stay awake. I didn't realise it but eventually, even in that position, I must have nodded off too because suddenly I was woken up by a loud banging and the sound of Shipley cursing! I was immediately concerned for Mom but realised that it was coming from Trev's room! I rubbed my eyes to see more clearly and looked at the clock, it was, 1.10am! I swung my legs out of bed and sat there listening frightened in case Jack went to Mom!

It was only a few minutes before I heard his bedroom door bursting open – banging back against the wall – followed by something falling over. My heart began to pound in my chest while Jack continued with his tirade of abuse. Coming ever closer to my bedroom door and then in his drunken rage, he banged and kicked at the door with such force that the whole casement rattled and the plaster cracked about the architraves! He screeched obscenities in an incoherent slur but fortunately, although the chest of drawers was rocked to and fro, the door held firm. He appeared to become exhausted by his efforts, then gradually the force and the noise receded. Having jumped from my bed I stood there, shaking nervously, behind the chest of drawers, with a shoe held firmly in my right hand, though what good this might have been God only knows but I had no need to discover. The silence became even more frightening than the preceding bombardment and perhaps this meant that I had no reason to act at all, but I did!

I pulled on my jeans and shirt and instead of cowering in a corner, I found myself gradually sliding the drawers to one side and turning the key slowly and silently in the lock. Then I slid the bolt, that I'd fitted just days earlier, gently backwards. Easing back the door not knowing what to expect, I eased it to a position where a crack of light pierced the room entering from the landing window. I could see his figure in the light and I saw that he had his back towards the door. He was swaying wearily on his feet. I tried to decipher the incoherent mumbling that he appeared to be making, but I could not. He stood between me and the stairs and he still did not turn as I slid the door open wider. Then, instinctively, and without any further consideration for the consequences, I swung with both hands wide and pressed firmly against the frame, lifting my legs into the air, and with all of my strength I kicked him with both feet in the middle of his lower back. I landed outstretched on my back upon the floor but saw Jack somersault through the air; downwards into the darkness of the stairs, before hitting the floor with a mighty thud.

It was a surreal moment that lasted a mere micro-second. As if in slow motion the whole process played within my head. The metallic clash of the radiator and pipes played like gigantic symbols against my brow. I sat and looked downwards briefly, there was no movement. Quickly I scurried down after him instinctively catching hold of my coat from the hooks above his slumped body and head. I twisted at the knob and pulled upon the door that was half-blocked by Jack's one outstretched leg. I struggled to open it. Then I heard the faintest of mumbles and, realising that he was still alive, I stooped to catch his words and I heard him clearly say that he had done for my Dad! Even now he still appeared to be mocking me! Just at that moment I heard a door open above, on the landing, and my Mother's voice. I squeezed out through the half-opened door, out into the night, and I ran with tears blinding my eyes and a burning anger in my heart. I ran and ran until that same heart that pounded within my chest felt as if it might burst, and always with that one hope, that he would die! Slowly I became aware of my own isolation and desperation, this present predicament and the consequences of my actions, and never had I felt so alone.

CHAPTER FOURTEEN
Reconstruction

The Second City development was now well underway; with vast swathes of the city being taken away, and then meticulously reconstructed. The site of the once thriving Irish Harp that had survived the onslaught of the German Luftwaffe was now nothing but rubble-strewn foundations. Sitting directly upon what would have been the position of the old snug – very often the scene of many a joyous; drunken celebration – was the gigantic, dinosaur-like, green and white MacAlpine crane. It towered above the city like something out of a Jules Verne novel; its mighty steel neck nodding to and fro and swinging frantically from side to side. From the steel chains that hung around its neck was suspended the mighty ball. This whooshed and crushed through the air and object, leaving destruction in its wake. Patrick Street, which had once been one of the pumping arteries amidst the city's heart, offered up no defence as the ball, like a surgeon's knife bisected and trisected its existence.

Harold Clyde was a meticulous, conscientious, Construction Site Inspector; his main responsibility, and object of being, was to ensure the safety of all those about him. Patrick Street had been cordoned off from three access points. 'Site Personnel Only' signs were in strategically placed positions. All of the site team wore blue hard hats and orange luminous jackets to ensure that any outside trespasser who encroached may be recognised immediately and quickly ushered away. During these times Harold took the responsibility upon his own shoulders for every individual; no one could enter or leave the site before reporting personally to him. He carried a clipboard with a check-list which was regularly updated and amended accordingly. Whenever the great ball was in motion Harold would constantly survey the terraces, usually just two properties ahead of its reach; his judgement was finite. Such times as these were always Harold's most anxious working moments. Harold was still very aware of the young man that he had come across only the other day; the one that had illegally and unwisely been squatting mid-terrace. It was his sincerest hope that the advice that he had then given had been accepted in the spirit in which it had been delivered. He had not seen the individual since and believed that he had vacated the scene.

This was not Harold's first chance meeting upon a squatter or squatters, and he acknowledged that, in such times of hardship, it would not be his last. There were many instances when he had had to deal with entire families who adamantly refused to leave their homes, even though every attempt by the local authority had been made to offer good alternative housing. But nothing these days stood in the way of progress. On this occasion though, the awareness of the presence of this one particular lad was somehow more relevant to him; this lad reminded him of young Michael, his nephew, who, at the age of 19, had tragically died in a motorcycle accident. This accident had only occurred six months earlier and had obviously had a great impact upon Harold. Of course it was only this young squatter's facial appearance where the resemblance lay, because his state of dress and personal appearance bore no resemblance.

As the ball swung constantly and ever closer to Harold's previous sighting, he became more anxious for his thoughts. He could not reflect upon why, because as usual, he had carried out his pre-inspection that morning with his normal due diligence. He always went in and out of every property before operations commenced. He clambered up every staircase, checked the loft spaces and every outbuilding. He was alert for any sign of occupation – food-stuffs or drink – and he would always call out at the top of his voice in order that any and every one might hear. Harold decided that the mid-terrace property still had time for one last check; he feared the responsibility of any tragic occurrence. He entered the property by pushing aside the ply-sheet security screen. He was certain that this was the property in question but he would check this and the next-door one. Harold took out from his inner pocket the little black note book where he recorded his daily jottings, as he crossed the small living room. Every property now had the appearance of any other. The previous remnants of occupation were in disarray or vandalised; nothing of any real value remained intact. He shouted loudly and listened carefully for the lightest of whispers, before clambering up the dark turn of the narrow stairway. Now his notebook was obscured from vision; along with the notes within. Suddenly the piercing light through the upstairs shutters penetrated the first bedroom. Harold picked his way carefully through the shafts of light in order to reach the second bedroom door. This was the room; he knew it. There before him was the filthy mattress lying upon the rubbish-strewn floor. The smell was offensive, and Harold immediately lifted a protective hand towards his mouth and nostrils.

Harold called out once more; he had no desire to delve amongst the rags. A sort of rag-bag of tangled junk heaped up in the centre was all that lay before him. He stepped begrudgingly closer and once more called out; ever aware that, outside, the swinging ball traversed toward him. No one answered. The lighting was very poor, with every shaft of scattered beam carrying the interspersed array of dust particles. Harold noticed an old stair spindle lying before his feet and so he bent to pick it up. He crossed the floor toward the window, stumbling slightly over an unseen fire fender. Several flies buzzed about his face; he brushed them quickly to one side. He raised the spindle, swung it backwards and battered the window shutter. Dust flew everywhere and Harold coughed out instinctively. The shutter was particularly stubborn but Harold was determined with his blows and eventually, after several vicious swipes, the shutter bounced from its fixing and swung downwardly to the floor. Light flooded in and illuminated the distasteful sight. Harold moved closer to the pile of rags; he could hear the pounding of the giant ball. He bent down and moved aside some old newspapers; a syringe needle rolled out across the boards and Harold flinched back, realising that he must be more cautious for his own welfare. He held back, momentarily considering whether or not to retire to safety, but something nagged at him, telling him he must not. He crouched down and pulled aside an old black dress; he jumped backwards and up in shock as a hand dropped limply from beneath it. The stench was obnoxious and he could not help but fear the worst. He reached into his coat pocket and pulled out his hanky, clutching it tightly across his nose and mouth. For a moment he considered the implications of his actions, should he be interfering with the scene of a crime. He thought once more about his lost nephew and could not help himself from carrying on. Slowly he raised an old donkey jacket; flies scattered upwardly and there, with shock, he saw the ashen face of that same youth.

Harold backed off, aware of the impending risks. He swiftly ran down the stairwell away from the stench, the filth and his horrible discovery. Harold thought that he might vomit and he staggered into the air and sunlight, screaming at the top of his voice: "STOP!-STOP!-STOP! For God's sake stop the ball!" It was obvious that the crane driver had not heard him, so Harold ran out into the road where he could see Arthur Roughton, a colleague of his, at the far end of the terrace. The ball swung on and he screamed; "ARTHUR-ARTHUR!" to his distant friend, who suddenly swung around recognising the distress in Harold's tone, and he in turn screamed out: "STOP THE BLOODY BALL!" The crane swung its jib upwardly and outwardly, therefore avoiding the next strike, and causing the ball to swipe aimlessly into mid-air.

"Arthur," he shouted, "I've found a body!"

Arthur drew nearer in response and several others came to see the reason for Harold's distress. The gangly Arthur Roughton was first at Harold's side and asked for him to repeat himself, hardly having believed his ears.

"That lad who I thought I'd moved on the other day; he's upstairs mid-terrace, it looks like he's a gonner, mate!"

"No! Are you certain?"

"I just came from up there and it's not a pretty sight; call an ambulance quickly mate and I'll let the others know what's happening."

***

The television was blasting away in the corner of the living room, with no one watching it, whilst in the kitchen, the steam blew sharply from the whistling kettle. Mrs Shipley (nee White) carefully placed thinly sliced tomato upon the ham lying on the buttered bread; she then poured the kettle out into the prepared mug before returning to the living-room, mug and plate in hand. The National News was just giving way to the Central News slot and the friendly figure of Bob Warman appeared upon the screen. Floss sat back down upon her corner comfy chair, placing herself before the TV. She listened to Bob relaying the local rail delay news, apparently due to necessary repairs on the track. He then moved seamlessly on to news of travellers who had moved unlawfully onto the local park; the local council spokesman explained that notice had been served for their eviction but that these things took time. Bob then announced that a newsflash had just reached his desk and that, apparently, during the demolition works at the Second City redevelopment site, the body of a young man had been discovered lying in one of the old terraced properties in Patrick Street. It had happened at a time when the terraces in question were being taken down. He stated that, at this moment, they had no further information but there would be an update in the next bulletin. Floss tutted to herself and rediscovered the sudden pangs of loss. Josh had been missing now for three years and there had been no sightings or police visits for a long period of time. She could not help but feel empathy for some other distressed parents loss.

Florence finished her lunch; switched off the television and then fetched out the ironing board from the rear lobby, where it was stored. She walked across and picked up the washing basket from its position alongside the washing machine, and went back to place it on the worktop next to the board. Carefully she picked her way through both hers and her son's clothing; pressing and folding. She stopped when she thought that she had heard a bell ring. She waited momentarily and then continued once more; but then she was sure that she had heard the bell and as she walked through the living room, it rang once more. When she entered into the hallway, she saw that there were two shadows, partially obliterating the sunshine from the glazed door. She quickly returned to the iron to switch it off, and then made her way hastily to the front door. There was a moment of hesitation at the door before she pulled it backwards towards her. As she opened the door she felt history repeating itself; there was an immediate flashback and a grinding, gnawing pain of discontentment. Her heart upped its beat because before her stood a policeman and a policewoman. It had been some time since police last stood on her doorstep. She remembered how Josh had called her to the door the night Frank had been killed.

Both of the officers appeared extremely young and seemed to have difficulty in delivering their message. Florence said hello, and the male officer asked quietly, "Are you Mrs Florence White?"

"Well actually it's Mrs Shipley now," she replied. Then she could no longer hold it back and she blurted out, "It's not my son, is it?"

The policewoman stepped forward and asked, "Do you mind if we come in Mrs Shipley?" Florence politely held back the door and both officers walked into the hall; they hesitated while Florence closed the door and let her go forward, leading them into the living room. She pointed to the sofa, and both officers removed their hats and sat down. The policeman began to explain that a youth had been found in a derelict terraced property in Patrick Street.

Mrs Shipley interrupted, "Yes I know; I just saw that, moments ago on Central News."

The policewoman then asked; "You mentioned a son at the door, where is he now, do you know?"

Mrs Shipley became unsure of the subject, "I have two sons," she said. "Trevor, the eldest, is at work, or should be; he works at the Spring Factory in Byron Street."

The officer said, "How about your second son, Mrs Shipley?"

Florence felt sick; she was getting hot and

uncomfortable realising that the subject of her missing son was about to be raised, and she feared the possibility of a conclusion. She moved restlessly to the edge of the seat; feeling as if she wanted to escape there and then, not wanting to be told the news she dreaded most. The change in her demeanour must have become very evident. The policewoman asked, "Are you alright Mrs Shipley?" She stood, and moved to Florence's side. She sat down upon the arm of the chair and clasped Florence's hand in hers.

Florence began to explain the situation to the rookie officers who, it appeared, had not been given the historical facts of the case. She explained that her youngest son, Josh, had gone missing some years earlier, on the same day that his step-father had unfortunately died. She advised that if they were to consult with their colleagues, they would find that there had been a period of family problems involving her eldest son as well and that her life had been upside down since the sudden death of her first husband. She knew that she was probably rambling on but she found it difficult to control her emotions, and she began to weep. The policewoman comforted her, whilst the other officer, who had taken his little notebook from his pocket, began to jot things down. When she was again able; Florence explained that Josh had now been gone for some years, and that lengthy police searches had failed in locating his whereabouts. Probably in an attempt to reduce the impact of the message that she now believed they had come to deliver, she added, "I suppose that I have to accept that I probably will never see him alive again." The policeman then asked if her youngest son had ever carried a pocket watch which had an inscription upon it. Florence immediately sobbed louder, and the policewoman again tried to comfort her. Eventually she was able to reply that her late first husband had carried a pocket watch that she had bought for him and that she had not seen it in many years. She then asked about the inscription. She heard her very own sentiments repeated; those that she had had lovingly engraved. She dropped her head into her hands and was inconsolable. The policewoman suggested that the other officer might call upon a neighbour to come to her side, so he went away and came back with Mrs Gould. Whilst Mrs Gould sat with Florence, the officers asked if they could make some tea for them, and Mrs Gould suggested that it might be for the best. She too had seen the news on the television but had not really attached the probable meaning to it. Once Florence had become more settled, it was suggested that she should go with them to The Queen Elizabeth Hospital, in the city. Florence immediately agreed, and Mrs Gould was asked if she might notify Mrs Shipley's elder son of the events.

The journey to the hospital took no longer than fifteen minutes and not a word was spoken during that time. The police car radio blurted out message after message and occasionally the officers returned the calls. Florence Shipley was in a daze; it mattered not one iota that no one acknowledged her. Her mind raced over and over the events of the last half an hour. She could not digest the turn and speed of such events that had now occurred, and which caused her throat to restrict and leave her breathless. Suddenly she was startled to hear her name being repeated over and over; Mrs Shipley, Mrs Shipley. She suddenly realised that the door of the car was being held open wide and that the policewoman was stooping to look in at her.

"Are you alright Mrs Shipley, or do you need a moment?"

Somewhat stunned, she answered, "Yes!"

Then as if she suddenly realised what was expected of her she repeated, "Yes! Yes!" And she stepped out of the car to the support of the police lady's helping hands.

Inside the hospital, she stood waiting; wringing her hands together as the police officers discussed matters at the reception desk. Then the WPC took her by her arm; smiled kindly and thoughtfully at her, and led her slowly away to a half glazed door marked, 'Private'. The door had only been a few short paces along the corridor but it had seemed to Florence to be much more. Her legs had become very heavy and slightly out of synchronisation. She felt very hot, faint and queasy. As the police officer had led her, she had felt the tightening grip of the hand around her arm whilst Florence had fiddled unwillingly and instinctively with the top button of her blouse. When she at last sat down in what appeared to be no more than a waiting room, the WPC crouched before her.

"Can I get you some water, Mrs Shipley; are you alright?"

"Yes I'm okay, is it warm in here? I feel very warm."

The police officer looked at her and smiled, "Yes it is warm, just you sit back comfortably and I'll get you that cold water."

When she returned with the water she asked, "Where did you say that your eldest son worked again, Mrs Shipley?"

Florence sipped at the water and replied. The police officer noted it down in her little pocketbook.

What, in reality was only a short period of time, seemed like an eternity as the male officer came, went and then returned. At times the young policeman would come and speak to the policewoman, and at times they would both leave Florence, for what was probably just minutes. There was a large round-faced wall clock immediately opposite to where Florence sat; it had large white fingers and ticked very loudly. Besides the occasional vehicle that passed by the window outside, the constant tick was the dominating sound. Upon his next return the policeman brought with him tea in polystyrene cups. There was no sugar in the tea and Florence always took two teaspoons, so it tasted very bitter to her. She could smell the regular hospital smells of bleach, disinfectant and other, more putrid smells. She was just finishing off her cup of bitter tea when the door opened and in walked Trevor. Florence, with a gesture, half stood up to meet him as he approached her; she had a sudden feeling of release, relief and happiness to see a recognisable face. She now had someone to share her experience with and to support her; the officers had been marvellous but this was better. She suddenly felt her eyes well up with tears and she wiped them from her face with the back of her hand. Trevor placed a loving arm around his Mom's shoulders; sitting down next to her, he pulled her closely to him to show that he was there for her. He smelled of oils and steel but Florence buried her head into his rough shirt.

"How long have you been here, Mom?"

"I don't really know; I've lost track of time."

"What's happening; why are you waiting, have they explained?"

"It's our Josh, Trevor. First I saw something on the telly but I didn't think too much on it, then next thing I know I've got the police stood at the front door."

"The copper who came for me said it was about my brother; I didn't understand, but all he'd say is that they'd found someone in an old terrace in Patrick Street. Oh! And he mentioned something about a watch as well."

"That Bob Warman on Central News said that a body of a young man had been found in Patrick Street, where they're demolishing and when the police came it suddenly all rushed back to me. I never, ever thought that I'd see this day; I thought, it's a mistake, but then they asked about the pocket-watch with the inscription."

Trevor looked at his Mom with grave concern; nothing was said for a moment. He saw a tear roll slowly down from her right eye, so he put his thumb to it and brushed it gently to one side. He now realised the gravity of this situation. What could he say? He too was tongue tied. He felt an overbearing pain. He struggled to bring the words to his lips.

"It'll be alright Mom; I'm here now. I've let you down too many times and I'll never do it again." He choked on his words.

Just as he had finished these words the door swung open behind them and the young policeman walked in. He crossed the room to where they both sat and said softly to them, "They're ready now Mrs Shipley; would you and your son please follow me?"

As they stood up Trevor held his Mom's right arm and he felt his Mother's legs slip slightly from beneath her, so he steadied her, then placed his arm around her, reassuring her that he was there. She was drained of colour and unsteady on her feet. They both followed the police constable diagonally across the outside corridor, entering into the open doors of the lift. The WPC stood inside holding the lift button. The doors closed slowly behind them, shutting out some of the intensity of light that was within the corridors. The lift went up two floors, during which time Trevor did not release his hold upon his Mom. It came to a sudden jerky stop, bouncing to a halt. The door slid backward and, once more, the light flooded in. Directly outside there was a man in a smart grey suit, who appeared to be waiting for them; he had a small dark moustache and that was all that really distinguished him. He smiled pleasantly and the policeman introduced him to them as, 'Detective Inspector Wilkins'. He leant slightly down toward them and shook Trevor firmly by the right hand. He asked them to follow him and led them across the corridor into a small vacant office. The Detective then offered them both a seat and the police constable kindly held a chair forward towards Mrs Shipley. Both of them reluctantly accepted their chairs, wondering what was to happen next. There were no doors off this office. The Detective sat to the other side of a desk that was over-stacked with files and documents. He leant backwards; half sitting upon his chair and, from a coat behind him, he reached out from the pocket a small white linen bag. It was no more than a stringed pouch. He pulled open the string top and opened it slowly, removing the contents from within. Florence reacted to this by reaching out to Trevor's hand and clutching firmly upon it.

Out came the silver pocket-watch. It had no chain attached; it was just a watch. Detective Inspector Wilkins slowly read the inscription.

"Did, or does, this watch belong to a member of your family?" he enquired.

Trevor immediately responded, "It's Dad's!"

Florence increased her grip upon her son's hand and said, "It was my late husband's watch."

"And would it be in the possession of anyone but your family?" the Detective enquired.

Trevor and his Mom looked at each other momentarily and she answered, "I believe that my youngest son would have had it in his possession, after he lost his Dad he very rarely let it go."

"Am I right in assuming the name of your youngest son to be Josh White, Mrs Shipley?"

"Yes!" Florence replied.

The Detective stood up from his chair, rounded the desk and went to speak to the young policeman standing next to the door, who immediately opened the door and left the room. The Detective then took another chair from alongside the wall and placed it just beside Florence. He sat there still clutching the watch within the palm of his right hand. Without speaking he offered the watch forward towards them. Florence did not move but Trevor reached forward to take it. He looked closely at the rubbed inscription; now not so visible as it once had been. Once, on that day in Cornwall, when he had first looked admiringly upon it, the engraved edges were sharp and crisp and you could feel it rubbing across your fingers. The memories came rushing back to him and he felt the need to pass the watch into his Mother's hands. She looked at it. It was a symbol from the past; the life that had drained from her since, so much happiness and too much misery. It represented 'LOVE'. The hurt was so intense that she immediately cried out loudly. She tottered upon her seat and seemed to fall forward but Trevor held her firmly.

The DI got to his feet and, from the rear of the desk, he offered forward a box of tissues, he pulled several from the top and passed these to Trevor. Florence had closed the watch tightly within her hand, and Trevor knelt down before her and tried to wipe away her tears but for a few moments she was inconsolable.

"Let it go, Mom; let it go, it's the past, we can't put things right, we're alright now we've got to think to the future." Trevor whispered to her.

Florence appeared to be repeating something and Trevor could not make out what she was saying, so he held her close to him and listened carefully.

"My babies! My babies!" he heard her keep repeating between the sobs.

By now the Detective had called the policewoman in to the room and she too tried to offer Florence her support. Trevor managed to gently remove the watch from his

Mother's grip and he handed it back to the Detective, who could only say, "I'm sorry." Then to Trevor he added quietly, "Of course someone may well have stolen the watch or it may even have been sold on." He then enquired, "How old would your brother have been now Mr White?"

Trevor replied without hesitation or cause to doubt, "Twenty-one; just recently he was twenty-one."

The door to the office opened again and the young policeman returned to speak quietly to the Detective. He then turned to Trevor and Florence and said, "They're ready for us now Mrs Shipley; do you think it for the best that your son should accompany us alone until you feel that you are ready?"

Trevor nodded; thinking to be doing the right thing for his Mother, but he felt her clutch tightly at his forearm.

"I want to see my son!" she spluttered out.

Trevor replied, "Perhaps it would be for the best, Mom?"

"No!" she repeated; "I want to see Josh!"

The WPC then asked, "Are you certain you will be okay, Mrs Shipley?"

Florence was determined and she began to stand; both the WPC and Trevor instinctively offered their support. Florence was not going to be deterred, so four of them left the office, leaving behind the WPC. The young constable led the way and pushed aside the double swing-doors allowing the others to pass him by and on into a large ward. They all walked towards the far end of the room with the Constable again taking the lead until they reached a single, cream painted door with large brass coloured plates fitted top and bottom; this had an oval window cut into the top centre. The Constable held this door open and allowed the others to pass by him into a small square room. Inside this room there were curtains fixed to a round brass pole;

hanging drawn-to, from floor to just below ceiling level. This room stank heavily of disinfectants and anaesthetics. All four stood together in one tight, huddled group. The curtain shook a little from movement inside and then it slid partly open. A tall man dressed in light green and whites came out and pulled the curtain closed behind him. Firstly he had a brief word with the DI, and then he pulled back the curtain once more. Florence felt the tightening of the restrictive knot that gripped upon her throat and she lifted a hand to her neck. Trevor felt her sag and immediately lifted her; the PC reacted similarly.

As they moved forward it was difficult to distinguish the diminutive shape upon the bed; that was tightly covered, wrapped in linen. A machine bleeped away noisily, and drip bottles were hung either side of the bed, with polythene tubes running from them down beneath the covers. Trevor was shocked! The Detective motioned him to come closer to the bedside, and the young policeman assisted Florence in her approach. The Detective then asked, "Is this your brother Mr White?"

Trevor was taken aback. Until now he had tried to restrain his tears in order to give his Mother the strength of his support but suddenly he openly wept. He was totally overawed; he could not believe the awful way in which his brother must have suffered to be in such a poor state. Florence clung once more tightly to his arm and there were audible gasps. Like feeling the sudden explosion of a huge dam, it was a sweeping rapture that immersed them and dragged them along with its torrents. Both he and his Mother wept. His tears flowed and his body ached. He had not expected to see this and neither had his Mom. It was all too much! The machine went on, 'bleep-bleep-bleep!' Trevor reached out his fingers to touch the wasted face. The bones were prominent, the eyes were dark and sunken and his complexion was ashen-pale; the hair was greasy-thin and long, the lips were split open and scabbed. He heard his Mother whisper the words, "Oh my God!" and then repeat, "Oh my God, what have they done to my son?" She too could not help herself from reaching forward to touch this face. Two chairs were pushed in behind them, and they were beckoned to sit down.

"You've answered my question; we'll leave you alone with your boy."

These were the words of the DI as he, the PC and the Surgeon left the room. Trevor and his Mom sat hand in hand at the bedside; they had not been brought to this room to identify the body. Josh was alive! For a few moments they just sat silently in disbelief, and looked upon this distressing but amazing sight. They watched as they saw flickers of movement from lips and eyes. How much they both desired to cradle Josh in their loving arms, to take away his pain and to bring back new life. Trevor heard the door move behind them and it opened a fraction. It was the doctor, who said quietly, "I'm sorry, but you only have about ten minutes, it's for his own good. If you could see him in a couple of hour's time he'll probably be more aware of you." He added, "I'll leave you alone a little but I'll return shortly."

Trevor nodded his thanks, acknowledging that he understood.

"Oh Trevor, look at him, look at my baby," Florence cried.

Trevor held her and comforted her, "He's alive Mom, that's all that's important. He's alive and he'll be good again; I know he will."

Both of them sat down next to Josh, fighting the emotion that stirred within them; neither spoke another word but just listened to the constant bleep and stared at the motionless figure.

They had not been there for more than five minutes when they heard a muffled sound from Josh; he seemed to be becoming a little more restless and disturbed, his lips quivered but he made no further noise. Trevor looked outside for the nurse and beckoned for her to return. Josh had become a little flushed in colour and the bleeping machine stepped up a pace. The nurse felt Josh's brow and inserted a thermometer between his lips.

***

Josh stood high upon his surfboard riding the waves, arms outstretched to maintain his balance, alongside his best friend Liam. The silvery rays of the noon sun shone down upon them, glinting off the peaks of the water and dazzling their vision. The salty spray continuously showered their faces as they glanced across at one another – each admiring the other's prowess – and they smiled happily. One almighty wave after another lifted them upwards into the sparse billowy clouds then dropped them swiftly into a downward splash. Josh waved to his friend and Liam waved back. Suddenly an enormous giant of a wave; like a cavorting lizard, threw them skywards, higher than ever, and they both found themselves wrapped up in a never-ending spiral of effervescent foam sinking into the depths. Josh surfaced, gasping for breath and clasping tightly upon his ankle restrainer as the board whipped about savagely. He looked anxiously about him, seeking out his friend in fear for his safety. Suddenly from out of nowhere, Liam appeared alongside him, clutching wildly at his pounding board. Josh called out to Liam and Liam in turn reassured his friend that all was fine but then once more he disappeared from view, as if he had been dragged downwards by some unseen force, back into the black depths. In anguish, Josh shouted out Liam's name repeatedly and, once more, Liam appeared back at his side. This time Liam assured Josh that all was well but that he now had to return. Josh did not understand; return where? So as Liam once more submerged he grabbed out wildly at his hand, and in that clutch he too was dragged below the surface and into the depths. The blinding sunlight disappeared from view, and blackness surrounded them both until a swirling ball of light penetrated the black void and enveloped Liam, whisking him away from Josh's reach. Suddenly as he struggled helplessly alone, Josh was thrown outwards and upwards across the waves, and the piercing sunlight returned. He found himself being tossed from the water, out onto the sands, and the last thing that he heard was his friend telling him, that it was time to let him go and climb back upon his board to once more ride high upon the waves.

***

The nurse urgently summoned for the doctor to return and Trevor and his Mom were asked to leave. They were both taken back to the office where the police waited once more to greet them and complete their work. Trevor was given a couple of sheets of written paper; his mind wasn't really with it, he didn't really care what they were for. He was aware that the detective had mumbled a few words to him; all he caught was that it was, "the necessary paperwork." It was offered up to him so he obligingly signed. Then the detective again produced the watch from the pouch and gave it a rough wipe over, before handing it once more to Trevor. Trevor passed it on to his Mom; who lovingly clasped it firmly in the palm of her hand. The detective stood up, shook Trevor's hand, thanked Florence for her help and then he and the PC stood at the doorway. His final words were to express hope that Josh would soon make a speedy recovery, and to assure them that they would only be needed at a later date if this was deemed necessary, although he may well need to speak with Josh at some stage about his whereabouts for the last few years, so that the missing persons case could be wrapped up. After they had left, the WPC re-entered the room and asked Mrs Shipley and Trevor if they were ready, and would they mind following her. A very heavy weight had been lifted from their shoulders and they were pleased to comply with any request that was made of them, so they willingly obliged. She took them along the corridor and introduced them to a stoutly built nurse and handed them over to what she called "her capable hands." She smiled kindly at both of them and then she left. The nurse, in turn, took a few details relating to Josh, and then delivered them into a small office where a red-faced Specialist sat. He advised them of Josh's state of health and suggested that they might, if they wished, leave now and return later, but they insisted on staying until they had seen Josh once more. The Specialist pressed a buzzer on his desk and the nurse returned, and they were both taken to a canteen two floors below, where the nurse advised them that as soon as Josh was awake they would be informed.

Trevor got two teas from the serving counter and then he joined his Mom where she sat by a window, overlooking a garden with a fish pond. It was tranquil, a pleasant oasis within an urban setting. There they both sat bewildered and shocked by the mixed emotions that they had been through coupled with their misunderstandings. The TV report had firstly triggered things, and then there was the way in which Florence had been brought to the hospital, definitely fearing for the worst. It had all been so very draining but now to have been reunited with Josh after all those lost years; they could not wait to be at his side once more, and to talk with him.

***

They had to wait patiently for a long while before suddenly the nurse approached them; her heels clipping across the stone tiles of the canteen floor. They were told they could return to Josh's bedside were the machinery still bleeped away and there appeared to have been little that had changed… except maybe that Josh looked, or seemed to look, more at ease and relaxed. Mrs White sat with Josh's frail left hand tenderly held within her own. It seemed to be some time before she sensed any acknowledgement of her touch but Josh momentarily seemed to tense and relax his fingers. Mrs White stared impatiently at his closed eyes and saw the minute flicker. She quickly sent Trevor for more tea, saying nothing of her belief that Josh was about to regain consciousness. As the curtain closed, she lowered her face next to Josh's and whispered, "You did not kill him!"

"Josh, can you hear me, you did not kill him! I stood on the landing and saw the door closing behind you, I called out your name but you didn't answer. Slowly I came down the stairs holding his baseball bat firmly in my right hand. When I reached his side I heard his mumbling and I heard him say, "I did for your Dad!" I swung the bat with such force against the rear of his drooping neck that I heard the crack and then I swung it a second time! He never moved again! I ran through to the kitchen, opened the door and threw the bat into the long grass at the back of the garden. When the ambulance came I told them that he had fallen down the stairs, that he was drunk and that I had heard the clang of metal! I heard the police constable talking to them and I heard them say that he had broken his neck in the fall, having struck the steel radiator with such force! They examined the radiator and they could see the blood and hair on it. I'm so sorry Josh, please forgive me."

The End